Elena looked up. "Stefan, I love you. But don't you understand, I have to choose for all of us to stay together. Just for now. *Do* you understand?" Seeing only stoniness in Stefan's face, she turned to Damon. "Do you?"

"I think so." He gave her a possessive smile. "I told Stefan from the beginning that he was selfish not to share you."

"That's not what I meant."

"Isn't it?" Damon smiled again.

"No," Stefan said. "*I* don't understand. He's evil, Elena. He kills for pleasure, he has no conscience at all—"

"Right now he's being more cooperative than you are," Elena said. "Stefan, do you really want to be mortal enemies with your brother forever?"

"Do you really think *he* wants anything else?"

Elena didn't answer for a minute, and when she did it was very quietly.

"He stopped me from killing you."

Elena felt the flare of Stefan's defensive anger, then felt it slowly fade. "Then you do agree?" she said quietly.

"Yes. I . . . agree."

"And *I* agree," said Damon, extending his hand with exaggerated courtesy. "In fact, we all seem to be in a frenzy of pure agreement."

Don't, Elena thought, but at that moment, standing in the cool twilight of the choir loft, she felt that it was true, that they were all three connected, and in accord, and strong.

D0253404

ALSO BY L.J. SMITH

THE VAMPIRE DIARIES

Volume I: *The Awakening*
Volume II: *The Struggle*
Volume III: *The Fury*
Volume IV: *Dark Reunion*

THE SECRET CIRCLE TRILOGY

Volume I: *The Initiation*
Volume II: *The Captive*
Volume III: *The Power*

The Night of the Solstice
Heart of Valor

Available from HarperPaperbacks

ATTENTION: ORGANIZATIONS AND CORPORATIONS

Most HarperPaperbacks are available at special quantity discounts for bulk purchases for sales promotions, premiums, or fund-raising. For information, please call or write:
Special Markets Department, HarperCollins Publishers,
10 East 53rd Street, New York, N.Y. 10022.
Telephone: (212) 207-7528. Fax: (212) 207-7222.

The Fury

Volume III

L. J. Smith

HarperPrism

A Division of HarperCollinsPublishers

HarperPrism
A Division of HarperCollins*Publishers*
10 East 53rd Street, New York, NY 10022–5299

This is a work of fiction. The characters, incidents, and dialogues are products of the author's imagination and are not to be construed as real. Any resemblance to actual events or persons, living or dead, is entirely coincidental.

A mass market edition of this book was published in 1991 by HarperPaperbacks.

Produced by Daniel Weiss Associates, Inc., 33 West 17th Street, New York, NY 10011.

HarperPrism printing: April 1999

Printed in the United States of America

ISBN 0-06-105991-9

Visit HarperPrism on the World Wide Web at
http://www.harpercollins.com

✦ 10 9 8 7 6 5 4 3 2

To my Aunt Margie, and in memory of
my Aunt Agnes and Aunt Eleanore,
for fostering creativity.

The Fury

One

Elena stepped into the clearing.

Beneath her feet tatters of autumn leaves were freezing into the slush. Dusk had fallen, and although the storm was dying away the woods were getting colder. Elena didn't feel the cold.

Neither did she mind the dark. Her pupils opened wide, gathering up tiny particles of light that would have been invisible to a human. She could see the two figures struggling beneath the great oak tree quite clearly.

One had thick dark hair, which the wind had churned into a tumbled sea of waves. He was slightly taller than the other, and although Elena couldn't see his face she somehow knew his eyes were green.

The other had a shock of dark hair as well, but his was fine and straight, almost like the pelt of an animal. His lips were drawn back from his teeth in fury, and the lounging grace of his body was gathered into a predator's crouch. His eyes were black.

Elena watched them for several minutes without moving. She'd forgotten why she had come here, why she'd been pulled here by the echoes of their battle in her mind. This close the clamor of their anger and hatred and pain was almost deafening, like silent shouts coming from the fighters. They were locked in a death match.

I wonder which of them will win, she thought. They were both wounded and bleeding, and the taller one's left arm hung at an unnatural angle. Still, he had just slammed the other against the gnarled trunk of an oak tree. His fury was so strong that Elena could feel and taste it as well as hear it, and she knew it was giving him impossible strength.

And then Elena remembered why she had come. How could she have forgotten? *He* was hurt. *His* mind had summoned her here, battering her with shock waves of rage and pain. She had come to help him because she belonged to him.

The two figures were down on the icy ground now, fighting like wolves, snarling. Swiftly and silently Elena went to them. The one with the wavy hair and green eyes—*Stefan*, a voice in her mind whispered—was on top, fingers scrabbling at the other's throat. Anger washed through Elena, anger and protectiveness. She reached between the two of them to grab that choking hand, to pry the fingers up.

It didn't occur to her that she shouldn't be strong enough to do this. She *was* strong enough; that was all. She threw her weight to the side, wrenching her captive away from his opponent. For good measure, she bore down hard on his wounded arm, knocking him flat on his face in the leaf-strewn slush. Then she began to choke him from behind.

Her attack had taken him by surprise, but he was far from beaten. He struck back at her, his good hand fumbling for her throat. His thumb dug into her windpipe.

Elena found herself lunging at the hand, going for it with her teeth. Her mind could not understand it, but her body knew what to do. Her teeth were a weapon, and they slashed into flesh, drawing blood.

But he was stronger than she was. With a

jerk of his shoulders, he broke her hold on him and twisted in her grasp, flinging her down. And then he was above her, his face contorted with animal fury. She hissed at him and went for his eyes with her nails, but he knocked her hand away.

He was going to kill her. Even wounded, he was by far the stronger. His lips had drawn back to show teeth already stained with scarlet. Like a cobra, he was ready to strike.

Then he stopped, hovering over her, his face changing.

Elena saw the green eyes widen. The pupils, which had been contracted to vicious dots, sprang open. He was staring down at her as if truly seeing her for the first time.

Why was he looking at her that way? Why didn't he just get it over with? But now the iron hand on her shoulder was releasing her. The animal snarl had disappeared, replaced by a look of bewilderment and wonder. He sat back, helping her to sit up, all the while gazing into her face.

"Elena," he whispered. His voice was cracked. "Elena, it's you."

Is that who I am? she thought. Elena?

It didn't really matter. She cast a glance toward the old oak tree. *He* was still there, standing between the upthrust roots, panting, supporting himself against it with one hand. *He* was looking at her with his endlessly black eyes, his brows drawn together in a frown.

Don't worry, she thought. I can take care of this one. He's stupid. Then she flung herself on the green-eyed one again.

"Elena!" he cried as she knocked him backward. His good hand pushed at her shoulder, holding her up. "Elena, it's me, Stefan! Elena, look at me!"

She was looking. All she could see was the exposed patch of skin at his neck. She hissed again, upper lip drawing back, showing him her teeth.

He froze.

She felt the shock reverberate through his body, saw his gaze shatter. His face went as white as if someone had struck him a blow in the stomach. He shook his head slightly on the muddy ground.

"No," he whispered. "Oh, no . . ."

He seemed to be saying it to himself, as if he didn't expect her to hear him. He reached a hand toward her cheek, and she snapped at it.

"Oh, Elena . . ." he whispered.

The last traces of fury, of animal bloodlust,

had disappeared from his face. His eyes were dazed and stricken and grieving.

And vulnerable. Elena took advantage of the moment to dive for the bare skin at his neck. His arm came up to fend her off, to push her away, but then it dropped again.

He stared at her a moment, the pain in his eyes reaching a peak, and then he simply gave up. He stopped fighting completely.

She could feel it happen, feel the resistance leave his body. He lay on the icy ground with scraps of oak leaves in his hair, staring up past her at the black and clouded sky.

Finish it, his weary voice said in her mind.

Elena hesitated for an instant. There was something about those eyes that called up memories inside her. Standing in the moonlight, sitting in an attic room. . . . But the memories were too vague. She couldn't get a grasp on them, and the effort made her dizzy and sick.

And this one had to die, this green-eyed one called Stefan. Because he'd hurt *him*, the other one, the one Elena had been born to be with. No one could hurt *him* and live.

She clamped her teeth into his throat and bit deep.

She realized at once that she wasn't doing

it quite right. She hadn't hit an artery or vein. She worried at the throat, angry at her own inexperience. It felt good to bite something, but not much blood was coming. Frustrated, she lifted up and bit again, feeling his body jerk in pain.

Much better. She'd found a vein this time, but she hadn't torn it deeply enough. A little scratch like that wouldn't do. What she needed was to rip it right across, to let the rich hot blood stream out.

Her victim shuddered as she worked to do this, teeth raking and gnawing. She was just feeling the flesh give way when hands pulled at her, lifting her from behind.

Elena snarled without letting go of the throat. The hands were insistent though. An arm looped about her waist, fingers twined in her hair. She fought, clinging with teeth and nails to her prey.

Let go of him. Leave him!

The voice was sharp and commanding, like a blast from a cold wind. Elena recognized it and stopped struggling with the hands that pulled her away. As they deposited her on the ground and she looked up to see *him*, a name came into her mind. Damon. *His* name was Damon. She stared at him sulkily, resentful of being yanked away from her kill, but obedient.

Stefan was sitting up, his neck red with blood. It was running onto his shirt. Elena licked her lips, feeling a throb like a hunger pang that seemed to come from every fiber of her being. She was dizzy again.

"I thought," Damon said aloud, "that you said she was dead."

He was looking at Stefan, who was even paler than before, if that was possible. That white face filled with infinite hopelessness.

"Look at her" was all he said.

A hand cupped Elena's chin, tilting her face up. She met Damon's narrowed dark eyes directly. Then long, slender fingers touched her lips, probing between them. Instinctively Elena tried to bite, but not very hard. Damon's finger found the sharp curve of a canine tooth, and Elena did bite now, giving it a nip like a kitten's.

Damon's face was expressionless, his eyes hard.

"Do you know where you are?" he said.

Elena glanced around. Trees. "In the woods," she said craftily, looking back at him.

"And who is that?"

She followed his pointing finger. "Stefan," she said indifferently. "Your brother."

"And who am I? Do you know who I am?"

She smiled up at him, showing him her pointed teeth. "Of course I do. You're Damon, and I love you."

Two

Stefan's voice was quietly savage. "That's what you wanted, wasn't it, Damon? And now you've got it. You had to make her like us, like you. It wasn't enough just to kill her."

Damon didn't glance back at him. He was looking at Elena intently through those hooded eyes, still kneeling there holding her chin. "That's the third time you've said that, and I'm getting a little tired of it," he commented softly. Disheveled, still slightly out of breath, he was yet self-composed, in control. "Elena, did I kill you?"

"Of course not," Elena said, winding her fingers in those of his free hand. She was getting impatient. What were they talking about anyway? Nobody had been killed.

11

"I never thought you were a liar," Stefan said to Damon, the bitterness in his voice unchanged. "Just about everything else, but not that. I've never heard you try to cover up for yourself before."

"In another minute," said Damon, "I'm going to lose my temper."

What more can you possibly do to me? Stefan returned. *Killing me would be a mercy.*

"I ran out of mercy for you a century ago," Damon said aloud. He let go, finally, of Elena's chin. "What do you remember about today?" he asked her.

Elena spoke tiredly, like a child reciting a hated lesson. "Today was the Founders' Day celebration." Flexing her fingers in his, she looked up at Damon. That was as far as she could get on her own, but it wasn't enough. Nettled, she tried to remember something else.

"There was someone in the cafeteria. . . . Caroline." She offered the name to him, pleased. "She was going to read my diary in front of everyone, and that was bad because . . ." Elena fumbled with the memory and lost it. "I don't remember why. But we tricked her." She smiled at him warmly, conspiratorially.

"Oh, 'we' did, did we?"

"Yes. You got it away from her. You did it for me." The fingers of her free hand crept under his jacket, searching for the square-cornered hardness of the little book. "Because you love me," she said, finding it and scratching at it lightly. "You do love me, don't you?"

There was a faint sound from the center of the clearing. Elena looked and saw that Stefan had turned his face away.

"Elena. What happened next?" Damon's voice called her back.

"Next? Next Aunt Judith started arguing with me." Elena pondered this a moment and at last shrugged. "Over . . . something. I got angry. She's not my mother. She can't tell me what to do."

Damon's voice was dry. "I don't think that's going to be a problem anymore. What next?"

Elena sighed heavily. "Next I went and got Matt's car. Matt." She said the name reflectively, flicking her tongue over her canine teeth. In her mind's eye, she saw a handsome face, blond hair, sturdy shoulders. "Matt."

"And where did you go in Matt's car?"

"To Wickery Bridge," Stefan said, turning back toward them. His eyes were desolate.

"No, to the boardinghouse," Elena corrected, irritated. "To wait for . . . mm . . . I forget. Anyway, I waited there. Then . . . then the storm started. Wind, rain, all that. I didn't like it. I got in the car. But something came after me."

"*Someone* came after you," said Stefan, looking at Damon.

"Some *thing*," Elena insisted. She had had enough of his interruptions. "Let's go away somewhere, just us," she said to Damon, kneeling up so that her face was close to his.

"In a minute," he said. "What kind of thing came after you?"

She settled back, exasperated. "I don't know what kind of thing! It was like nothing I've ever seen. Not like you and Stefan. It was . . ." Images rippled through her mind. Mist flowing along the ground. The wind shrieking. A shape, white, enormous, looking as if it were made out of mist itself. Gaining on her like a wind-driven cloud.

"Maybe it was just part of the storm," she said. "But I thought it wanted to hurt me. I got away though." Fiddling with the zipper to Damon's leather jacket, she smiled secretly and looked up at him through her lashes.

For the first time, Damon's face showed

14

emotion. His lips twisted in a grimace. "You got away."

"Yes. I remembered what . . . someone . . . told me about running water. Evil things can't cross it. So I drove toward Drowning Creek, toward the bridge. And then . . ." She hesitated, frowning, trying to find a solid memory in the new confusion. Water. She remembered water. And someone screaming. But nothing else. "And then I crossed it," she concluded finally, brightly. "I must have, because here I am. And that's all. Can we go now?"

Damon didn't answer her.

"The car's still in the river," said Stefan. He and Damon were looking at each other like two adults having a discussion over the head of an uncomprehending child, their hostilities suspended for the moment. Elena felt a surge of annoyance. She opened her mouth, but Stefan was continuing. "Bonnie and Meredith and I found it. I went underwater and got her, but by then . . ."

By then, what? Elena frowned.

Damon's lips were curved mockingly. "And you gave up on her? You, of all people, should have suspected what might happen. Or was the idea so repugnant to you that you couldn't even consider it? Would you rather she were really dead?"

"She had no pulse, no respiration!" Stefan flared. "And she'd never had enough blood to change her!" His eyes hardened. "Not from *me* anyway."

Elena opened her mouth again, but Damon laid two fingers on it to keep her quiet. He said smoothly, "And that's the problem now —or are you too blind to see that, too? You told me to look at her; look at her yourself. She's in shock, irrational. Oh, yes, even I admit that." He paused for a blinding smile before going on. "It's more than just the normal confusion after changing. She'll need blood, human blood, or her body won't have the strength to finish the change. She'll die."

What do you mean irrational? Elena thought indignantly. "I'm fine," she said around Damon's fingers. "I'm tired, that's all. I was going to sleep when I heard you two fighting, and I came to help you. And then you wouldn't even let me kill him," she finished, disgusted.

"Yes, why didn't you?" said Stefan. He was staring at Damon as if he could bore holes through him with his eyes. Any trace of cooperation on his part was gone. "It would have been the easiest thing to do."

Damon stared back at him, suddenly furious, his own animosity flooding up to meet Stefan's. He was breathing quickly and lightly. "Maybe I don't like things easy," he hissed. Then he seemed to regain control of himself once more. His lips curled in mockery, and he added, "Put it this way, dear brother: if anyone's going to have the satisfaction of killing you, it will be me. No one else. I plan to take care of the job personally. And it's something I'm very good at; I promise you."

"You've shown us that," Stefan said quietly, as if each word sickened him.

"But this one," Damon said, turning to Elena with glittering eyes, "I *didn't* kill. Why should I? I could have changed her any time I liked."

"Maybe because she had just gotten engaged to marry someone else."

Damon lifted Elena's hand, still twined with his. On the third finger a gold ring glittered, set with one deep blue stone. Elena frowned at it, vaguely remembering having seen it before. Then she shrugged and leaned against Damon wearily.

17

"Well, now," Damon said, looking down at her, "that doesn't seem to be much of a problem, does it? I think she may have been glad to forget you." He looked up at Stefan with an unpleasant smile. "But we'll find out once she's herself again. We can ask her then which of us she chooses. Agreed?"

Stefan shook his head. "How can you even suggest that? After what happened . . ." His voice trailed off.

"With Katherine? I can say it, if you can't. Katherine made a foolish choice, and she paid the price for it. Elena is different; she knows her own mind. But it doesn't matter if you agree," he added, overriding Stefan's new protests. "The fact is that she's weak now, and she needs blood. I'm going to see that she gets it, and then I'm going to find who did this to her. You can come or not. Suit yourself."

He stood, drawing Elena up with him. "Let's go."

Elena came willingly, pleased to be moving. The woods were interesting at night; she'd never noticed that before. Owls were sending their mournful, haunting cries through the trees, and deer mice scuttled away from her gliding feet. The air was colder in patches, as it froze first in the hollows and dips of the wood. She found it was easy to move silently beside Damon through the leaf litter; it was just a matter of being careful where she stepped. She didn't look back to see if Stefan was following them.

She recognized the place where they left the wood. She had been there earlier today. Now, however, there was some sort of frenzied activity going on: red and blue lights flashing on cars, spotlights framing the dark huddled shapes of people. Elena looked at them curiously. Several were familiar. That woman, for instance, with the thin harrowed face and the anxious eyes—Aunt Judith? And the tall man beside her—Aunt Judith's fiancé, Robert?

There should be someone else with them, Elena thought. A child with hair as pale as Elena's own. But try as she might, she could not conjure up a name.

The two girls with their arms around each other, standing in a circle of officials, *those* two she remembered though. The little red-haired one who was crying was Bonnie. The taller one with the sweep of dark hair, Meredith.

"But she's not *in* the water," Bonnie was saying to a man in a uniform. Her voice trembled on the edge of hysteria. "We saw Stefan get her out. I've told you and told you."

"And you left him here with her?"

"We had to. The storm was getting worse, and there was something coming—"

"Never mind that," Meredith broke in. She sounded only slightly calmer than Bonnie. "Stefan said that if he—had to leave her, he'd leave her lying under the willow trees."

"And just where is Stefan now?" another uniformed man asked.

"We don't know. We went back to get help. He probably followed us. But as for what happened to—to Elena . . ." Bonnie turned back and buried her face in Meredith's shoulder.

They're upset about *me*, Elena realized. How silly of them. I can clear that up, anyway. She started forward into the light, but Damon pulled her back. She looked at him, wounded.

"Not like that. Pick the ones you want, and we'll draw them out," he said.

"Want for what?"

"For feeding, Elena. You're a hunter now. Those are your prey."

Elena pushed her tongue against a canine

tooth doubtfully. Nothing out there looked like food to her. Still, because Damon said so, she was inclined to give him the benefit of the doubt. "Whichever you think," she said obligingly.

Damon tilted his head back, eyes narrowed, scanning the scene like an expert evaluating a famous painting. "Well, how about a couple of nice paramedics?"

"*No,*" said a voice behind them.

Damon barely glanced over his shoulder at Stefan. "Why not?"

"Because there've been enough attacks. She may need human blood, but she doesn't have to hunt for it." Stefan's face was shut and hostile, but there was an air of grim determination about him.

"There's another way?" Damon asked ironically.

"You know there is. Find someone who's willing—or who can be influenced to be willing. Someone who would do it for Elena and who is strong enough to deal with this, mentally."

"And I suppose you know where we can find such a paragon of virtue?"

"Bring her to the school. I'll meet you there," Stefan said, and disappeared.

They left the activity still bustling, lights flashing, people milling. As they went, Elena noticed a strange thing. In the middle of the river, illuminated by the spotlights, was an automobile. It was completely submerged except for the front fender, which stuck out of the water.

What a stupid place to park a car, she thought, and followed Damon back into the woods.

Stefan was beginning to feel again.

It hurt. He'd thought he was through with hurting, through with feeling anything. When he'd pulled Elena's lifeless body out of the dark water, he'd thought that nothing could ever hurt again because nothing could match that moment.

He'd been wrong.

He stopped and stood with his good hand braced against a tree, head down, breathing deeply. When the red mists cleared and he could see again, he went on, but the burning ache in his chest continued undiminished. Stop thinking about her, he told himself, knowing that it was useless.

But she wasn't truly dead. Didn't that count for something? He'd thought he would never hear her voice again, never feel her touch. . . .

And now, when she touched him, she wanted to kill him.

He stopped again, doubling over, afraid he was going to be sick.

Seeing her like this was worse torture than seeing her lying cold and dead. Maybe that was why Damon had let him live. Maybe this was Damon's revenge.

And maybe Stefan should just do what he'd planned to do after killing Damon. Wait until dawn and take off the silver ring that protected him from sunlight. Stand bathing in the fiery embrace of those rays until they burned the flesh from his bones and stopped the pain once and for all.

But he knew he wouldn't. As long as Elena walked the earth, he would never leave her. Even if she hated him, even if she hunted him. He would do anything he could to keep her safe.

Stefan detoured toward the boardinghouse. He needed to clean up before he could let humans see him. In his room, he washed the blood from his face and neck and examined his arm. The healing process had already begun, and with concentration he could accelerate it still further. He was burning up his Powers fast; the fight with his brother had already weakened him. But this was important. Not because of the pain—he scarcely noticed that—but because he needed to be fit.

Damon and Elena were waiting outside the school. He could feel his brother's impatience and Elena's wild new presence there in the dark.

"This had better work," Damon said.

Stefan said nothing. The school auditorium was another center of commotion. People ought to have been enjoying the Founders' Day dance; in fact, those who had remained through the storm were pacing around or gathered in small groups talking. Stefan looked in the open door, searching with his mind for one particular presence.

He found it. A blond head was bent over a table in the corner.

Matt.

Matt straightened and looked around, puzzled. Stefan willed him to come outside. *You need some fresh air,* he thought, insinuating the suggestion into Matt's subconscious. *You feel like just stepping out for a moment.*

To Damon, standing invisible just beyond the light, he said, *Take her into the school, to the photography room. She knows where it is. Don't show yourselves until I say.* Then he backed away and waited for Matt to appear.

Matt came out, his drawn face turned up to the moonless sky. He started violently when Stefan spoke to him.

"Stefan! You're here!" Desperation, hope, and horror struggled for dominance on his face. He hurried over to Stefan. "Did they—bring her back yet? Is there any news?"

"What have *you* heard?"

Matt stared at him a moment before answering. "Bonnie and Meredith came in saying that Elena had gone off of Wickery Bridge in my car. They said that she . . ." He paused and swallowed. "Stefan, it's not true, is it?" His eyes were pleading.

Stefan looked away.

"Oh, God," Matt said hoarsely. He turned his back on Stefan, pressing the heels of his hands into his eyes. "I don't believe it; I *don't*. It can't be true."

"Matt . . ." He touched the other boy's shoulder.

"I'm sorry." Matt's voice was rough and ragged. "You must be going through hell, and here I am making it worse."

More than you know, thought Stefan, his

hand falling away. He'd come with the intention of using his Powers to persuade Matt. Now that seemed an impossibility. He couldn't do it, not to the first—and only—human friend he'd had in this place.

His only other option was to tell Matt the truth. Let Matt make his own choice, knowing everything.

"If there were something you could do for Elena right now," he said, "would you do it?"

Matt was too lost in emotion to ask what kind of idiotic question that was. "Anything," he said almost angrily, rubbing a sleeve over his eyes. "I'd do anything for her." He looked at Stefan with something like defiance, his breathing shaky.

Congratulations, Stefan thought, feeling the sudden yawning pit in his stomach. You've just won yourself a trip to the Twilight Zone.

"Come with me," he said. "I've got something to show you."

Three

Elena and Damon were waiting in the darkroom. Stefan could sense their presence in the small annex as he pushed the door to the photography room open and led Matt inside.

"These doors are supposed to be locked," Matt said as Stefan flipped on the light switch.

"They were," said Stefan. He didn't know what else to say to prepare Matt for what was coming. He'd never deliberately revealed himself to a human before.

He stood, quietly, until Matt turned and looked at him. The classroom was cold and silent, and the air seemed to hang heavily. As the moment stretched out, he saw Matt's expression slowly change from grief-numbed bewilderment to uneasiness.

"I don't understand," Matt said.

"I know you don't." He went on looking at Matt, purposefully dropping the barriers that concealed his Powers from human perception. He saw the reaction in Matt's face as uneasiness coalesced into fear. Matt blinked and shook his head, his breath coming quicker.

"What—?" he began, his voice gravelly.

"There are probably a lot of things you've wondered about me," Stefan said. "Why I wear sunglasses in strong light. Why I don't eat. Why my reflexes are so fast."

Matt had his back to the darkroom now. His throat jerked as if he were trying to swallow. Stefan, with his predator's senses, could hear Matt's heart thudding dully.

"No," Matt said.

"You *must* have wondered, must have asked yourself what makes me so different from everybody else."

"No. I mean—I don't care. I keep out of things that aren't my business." Matt was edging toward the door, his eyes darting toward it in a barely perceptible movement.

"Don't, Matt. I don't want to hurt you, but

I can't let you leave now." He could feel barely leashed need emanating from Elena in her concealment. *Wait*, he told her.

Matt went still, giving up any attempt to move away. "If you want to scare me, you have," he said in a low voice. "What else do you want?"

Now, Stefan told Elena. He said to Matt, "Turn around."

Matt turned. And stifled a cry.

Elena stood there, but not the Elena of that afternoon, when Matt had last seen her. Now her feet were bare beneath the hem of her long dress. The thin folds of white muslin that clung to her were caked with ice crystals that sparkled in the light. Her skin, always fair, had a strange wintry luster to it, and her pale gold hair seemed overlaid with a silvery sheen. But the real difference was in her face. Those deep blue eyes were heavy-lidded, almost sleepy looking, and yet unnaturally awake. And a look of sensual anticipation and hunger curled about her lips. She was more beautiful than she had been in life, but it was a frightening beauty.

As Matt stared, paralyzed, Elena's pink tongue came out and licked her lips.

"Matt," she said, lingering over the first consonant of the name. Then she smiled.

Stefan heard Matt's indrawn breath of disbelief, and the near sob he gave as he finally backed away from her.

It's all right, he said, sending the thought to Matt on a surge of Power. As Matt jerked toward him, eyes wide with shock, he added, "So now you know."

Matt's expression said that he didn't want to know, and Stefan could see the denial in his face. But Damon stepped out beside Elena and moved a little to the right, adding his presence to the charged atmosphere of the room.

Matt was surrounded. The three of them closed in on him, inhumanly beautiful, innately menacing.

Stefan could smell Matt's fear. It was the helpless fear of the rabbit for the fox, the mouse for the owl. And Matt was right to be afraid. They were the hunting species; he was the hunted. Their job in life was to kill him.

And just now instincts were getting out of control. Matt's instinct was to panic and run, and it was triggering reflexes in Stefan's head. When the prey ran, the predator gave chase; it was as simple as that. All three of the predators here were keyed up, on edge, and Stefan felt he couldn't be responsible for the consequences if Matt bolted.

We don't want to harm you, he told Matt. *It's Elena who needs you, and what she needs won't leave you permanently damaged. It doesn't even have to hurt, Matt.* But Matt's muscles were still tensed to flee, and Stefan realized that the three of them were stalking him, moving closer, ready to cut off any escape.

You said you would do anything for Elena, he reminded Matt desperately and saw him make his choice.

Matt released his breath, the tension draining from his body. "You're right; I did," he whispered. He visibly braced himself before he continued. "What does she need?"

Elena leaned forward and put a finger on Matt's neck, tracing the yielding ridge of an artery.

"Not that one," Stefan said quickly. "You don't want to kill him. Tell her, Damon." He added, when Damon made no effort to do so, *Tell her.*

"Try here, or here." Damon pointed with clinical efficiency, holding Matt's chin up. He was strong enough that Matt couldn't break the grip, and Stefan felt Matt's panic surge up again.

Trust me, Matt. He moved in behind the human boy. *But it has to be your choice*, he finished, suddenly washed with compassion. *You can change your mind.*

Matt hesitated and then spoke through clenched teeth. "No. I still want to help. I want to help you, Elena."

"Matt," she whispered, her heavy-lashed jewel blue eyes fixed on his. Then they trailed down to his throat and her lips parted hungrily. There was no sign of the uncertainty she'd shown when Damon suggested feeding off the paramedics. "Matt." She smiled again, and then she struck, swift as a hunting bird.

Stefan put a flattened hand against Matt's back to give him support. For a moment, as Elena's teeth pierced his skin, Matt tried to recoil, but Stefan thought swiftly, *Don't fight it; that's what causes the pain.*

As Matt tried to relax, unexpected help came from Elena, who was radiating the warm happy thoughts of a wolf cub being fed. She had gotten the biting technique right on the first try this time, and she was filled with innocent pride and growing satisfaction as the sharp pangs of hunger eased. And with appreciation for Matt, Stefan realized, with a sudden shock of jealousy. She didn't hate Matt or want to kill him, because he posed no threat to Damon. She was fond of Matt.

Stefan let her take as much as was safe and then intervened. *That's enough, Elena. You don't want to injure him.* But it took the combined efforts of him, Damon, and a rather groggy Matt to pry her off.

"She needs to rest now," Damon said. "I'm taking her someplace where she can do it safely." He wasn't asking Stefan; he was telling him.

As they left, his mental voice added, for Stefan's ears alone, *I haven't forgotten the way you attacked me, brother. We'll talk about that later.*

Stefan stared after them. He'd noted how Elena's eyes remained locked on Damon, how she followed him without question. But she was out of danger now; Matt's blood had given her the strength she needed. That was all Stefan had to hang on to, and he told himself it was all that mattered.

He turned to take in Matt's dazed expression. The human boy had sunk into one of the plastic chairs and was gazing straight ahead.

Then his eyes lifted to Stefan's, and they regarded each other grimly.

"So," Matt said. "Now I know." He shook his head, turning away slightly. "But I still can't believe it," he muttered. His fingers pressed gingerly at the side of his neck, and he winced. "Except for this." Then he frowned. "That guy—Damon. Who is he?"

"My older brother," Stefan said without emotion. "How do you know his name?"

"He was at Elena's house last week. The kitten spat at him." Matt paused, clearly remembering something else. "And Bonnie had some kind of psychic fit."

"She had a precognition? What did she say?"

"She said—she said that Death was in the house."

Stefan looked at the door Damon and Elena had passed through. "She was right."

"Stefan, what's going on?" A note of appeal had entered Matt's voice. "I still don't understand. What's happened to Elena? Is she going to be like this forever? Isn't there anything we can do?"

"Be like what?" Stefan said brutally. "Disoriented? A vampire?"

Matt looked away. "Both."

"As for the first, she may become more rational now that she's fed. That's what Damon thinks anyway. As for the other, there's only one thing you can do to change her condition." As Matt's eyes lit with hope, Stefan continued. "You can get a wooden stake and hammer it through her heart. Then she won't be a vampire anymore. She'll just be dead."

Matt got up and went to the window.

"You wouldn't be killing her, though, because that's already been done. She drowned in the river, Matt. But because she'd had enough blood from me"—he paused to steady his voice—"and, it seems, from my brother, she changed instead of simply dying. She woke up a hunter, like us. That's what she'll be from now on."

With his back still turned, Matt answered. "I always knew there was something about you. I told myself it was just because you were from another country." He shook his head again self-deprecatingly. "But deep down I knew it was more than that. And something still kept telling me I could trust you, and I did."

"Like when you went with me to get the vervain."

"Yeah. Like that." He added, "Can you tell me what the hell it was for, now?"

"For Elena's protection. I wanted to keep Damon away from her. But it looks as if that's not what *she* wanted after all." He couldn't help the bitterness, the raw betrayal, in his voice.

Matt turned. "Don't judge her before you know all the facts, Stefan. That's one thing I've learned."

Stefan was startled; then, he gave a small humorless smile. As Elena's exes, he and Matt were in the same position now. He wondered if he would be as gracious about it as Matt had been. Take his defeat like a gentleman.

He didn't think so.

Outside, a noise had begun. It was inaudible to human ears, and Stefan almost ignored it—until the words penetrated his consciousness.

Then he remembered what he had done in this very school only a few hours ago. Until that moment, he'd forgotten all about Tyler Smallwood and his tough friends.

Now that memory had returned; shame and horror closed his throat. He'd been out of his mind with grief over Elena, and his reason had snapped under the pressure. But that was no excuse for what he had done. Were they all dead? Had he, who had sworn so long ago never to kill, killed six people today?

"Stefan, wait. Where are you going?" When he didn't answer, Matt followed him, half running to keep up, out of the main school building and onto the blacktop. On the far side of the field, Mr. Shelby stood by the Quonset hut.

The janitor's face was gray and furrowed with lines of horror. He seemed to be trying to shout, but only small hoarse gasps came out of his mouth. Elbowing past him, Stefan looked into the room and felt a curious sense of déjà vu.

It looked like the Mad Slasher room from the Haunted House fundraiser. Except that this was no tableau set up for visitors. This was real.

Bodies were sprawled everywhere, amid shards of wood and glass from the shattered window. Every visible surface was spattered with blood, red-brown and sinister as it dried. And one look at the bodies revealed why: each one had a pair of livid purple wounds in the neck. Except Caroline's: her neck was unmarked, but her eyes were blank and staring.

Behind Stefan, Matt was hyperventilating. "Stefan, Elena didn't—she didn't—"

"Be quiet," Stefan answered tersely. He glanced back at Mr. Shelby, but the janitor had stumbled over to his cart of brooms and mops and was leaning against it. Glass grated under Stefan's feet as he crossed the floor to kneel by Tyler.

Not dead. Relief exploded over Stefan at the realization. Tyler's chest moved feebly, and when Stefan lifted the boy's head his eyes opened a slit, glazed and unfocused.

You don't remember anything, Stefan told him mentally. Even as he did it, he wondered why he was bothering. He should just leave Fell's Church, cut out now and never come back.

But he wouldn't. Not as long as Elena was here.

He gathered the unconscious minds of the other victims into his mental grasp and told them the same thing, feeding it deep into their brains. *You don't remember who attacked you. The whole afternoon is a blank.*

As he did, he felt his mental Powers tremble like overfatigued muscles. He was close to burnout.

Outside, Mr. Shelby had found his voice at last and was shouting. Wearily, Stefan let

Tyler's head slip back through his fingers to the floor and turned around.

Matt's lips were peeled back, his nostrils flared, as if he had just smelled something disgusting. His eyes were the eyes of a stranger. "Elena didn't," he whispered. "*You* did."

Be quiet! Stefan pushed past him into the thankful coolness of the night, putting distance between him and that room, feeling the icy air on his hot skin. Running footsteps from the vicinity of the cafeteria told him that some humans had heard the janitor's cries at last.

"You did it, didn't you?" Matt had followed Stefan out to the field. His voice said he was trying to understand.

Stefan rounded on him. "Yes, I did it," he snarled. He stared Matt down, concealing none of the angry menace in his face. "I told you, Matt, we're hunters. Killers. You're the sheep; we're the wolves. And Tyler has been asking for it every day since I came here."

"Asking for a punch in the nose, sure. Like you gave him before. But—that?" Matt closed in on him, standing eye to eye, unafraid. He had physical courage; Stefan had to give him that. "And you're not even sorry? You don't even regret it?"

"Why should I?" said Stefan coldly, emptily. "Do you regret it when you eat too much steak? Feel sorry for the cow?" He saw Matt's look of sick disbelief and pressed on, driving the pain in his chest deeper. It was better that Matt stay away from him from now on, far away. Or Matt might end up like those bodies in the Quonset hut. "I am what I am, Matt. And if you can't handle it, you'd better steer clear of me."

Matt stared at him a moment longer, the sick disbelief transforming slowly into sick disillusionment. The muscles around his jaw stood out. Then, without a word, he turned on his heel and walked away.

Elena was in the graveyard.

Damon had left her there, exhorting her to stay until he came back. She didn't want to sit still, though. She felt tired but not really sleepy, and the new blood was affecting her like a jolt of caffeine. She wanted to go exploring.

The graveyard was full of activity although there wasn't a human in sight. A fox slunk through the shadows toward the river path. Small rodents tunneled under the long lank grass around the headstones, squeaking and scurrying. A barn owl flew almost silently toward the ruined church, where it alighted on the belfry with an eerie cry.

Elena got up and followed it. This was much better than hiding in the grass like a mouse or vole. She looked around the ruined church interestedly, using her sharpened senses to examine it. Most of the roof had fallen in, and only three walls were standing, but the belfry stood up like a lonely monument in the rubble.

At one side was the tomb of Thomas and Honoria Fell, like a large stone box or coffin. Elena gazed earnestly down into the white marble faces of their statues on the lid. They lay in tranquil repose, their eyes shut, their hands folded on their breasts. Thomas Fell looked serious and a little stern, but Honoria looked merely sad. Elena thought absently of her own parents, lying side by side down in the modern cemetery.

I'll go home; that's where I'll go, she thought. She had just remembered about home. She could picture it now: her pretty bedroom with blue curtains and cherrywood furniture and her little fireplace. And something important under the floorboards in the closet.

She found her way to Maple Street by instincts that ran deeper than memory, letting her feet guide her there. It was an old, old house, with a big front porch and floor-to-ceiling windows in front. Robert's car was parked in the driveway.

Elena started for the front door and then stopped. There was a reason people shouldn't see her, although she couldn't remember what it was right now. She hesitated and then nimbly climbed the quince tree up to her bedroom window.

But she wasn't going to be able to get in here without being noticed. A woman was sitting on the bed with Elena's red silk kimono in her lap, staring down at it. Aunt Judith. Robert was standing by the dresser, talking to her. Elena found that she could pick up the murmur of his voice even through the glass.

". . . out again tomorrow," he was saying. "As long as it doesn't storm. They'll go over every inch of those woods, and they'll find her, Judith. You'll see." Aunt Judith said nothing, and he went on, sounding more desperate. "We can't give up hope, no matter what the girls say—"

"It's no good, Bob." Aunt Judith had

raised her head at last, and her eyes were red-rimmed but dry. "It's no use."

"The rescue effort? I won't have you talking that way." He came over to stand beside her.

"No, not just that . . . although I know, in my heart, that we're not going to find her alive. I mean . . . everything. Us. What happened today is our fault—"

"That's not true. It was a freak accident."

"Yes, but we made it happen. If we hadn't been so harsh with her, she would never have driven off alone and been caught in the storm. No, Bob, don't try to shut me up; I want you to listen." Aunt Judith took a deep breath and continued. "It wasn't just today, either. Elena's been having problems for a long time, ever since school started, and somehow I've let the signs slip right past me. Because I've been too involved with myself—with *us*—to pay attention to them. I can see that now. And now that Elena's . . . gone . . . I don't want the same thing to happen with Margaret."

"What are you saying?"

"I'm saying that I can't marry you, not as soon as we planned. Maybe not ever." Without looking at him, she spoke softly.

43

"Margaret has lost too much already. I don't want her to feel she's losing me, too."

"She won't be losing you. If anything, she'll be gaining someone, because I'll be here more often. You know how I feel about her."

"I'm sorry, Bob; I just don't see it that way."

"You can't be serious. After all the time I've spent here—after all I've done . . ."

Aunt Judith's voice was drained and implacable. "I *am* serious."

From her perch outside the window, Elena eyed Robert curiously. A vein throbbed in his forehead, and his face had flushed red.

"You'll feel differently tomorrow," he said.

"No, I won't."

"You don't mean it—"

"I *do* mean it. Don't tell me that I'm going to change my mind, because I'm not."

For an instant, Robert looked around in helpless frustration; then, his expression darkened. When he spoke, his voice was flat and cold. "I see. Well, if that's your final answer, I'd better leave right now."

"Bob." Aunt Judith turned, startled, but he was already outside the door. She stood up, wavering, as if she were unsure whether or not to go after him. Her fingers kneaded at the red material she was holding. "Bob!" she called again, more urgently, and she turned to drop the kimono on Elena's bed before following him.

But as she turned she gasped, a hand flying to her mouth. Her whole body stiffened. Her eyes stared into Elena's through the silvery pane of glass. For a long moment, they stared at each other that way, neither moving. Then Aunt Judith's hand came away from her mouth, and she began to shriek.

Four

Something yanked Elena out of the tree and, yowling a protest, she fell and landed on her feet like a cat. Her knees hit the ground a second later and got bruised.

She reared back, fingers hooked into claws to attack whoever had done it. Damon slapped her hand away.

"Why did you grab me?" she demanded.

"Why didn't you stay where I put you?" he snapped.

They glared at each other, equally furious. Then Elena was distracted. The shrieking was still going on upstairs, augmented now by rattling and banging at the window. Damon nudged her against the house, where they couldn't be seen from above.

"Let's get away from this noise," he said fastidiously, looking up. Without waiting for a response, he caught her arm. Elena resisted.

"I have to go in there!"

"You can't." He gave her a wolfish smile. "I mean that literally. You *can't* go in that house. You haven't been invited."

Momentarily nonplussed, Elena let him tow her a few steps. Then she dug her heels in again.

"But I need my diary!"

"What?"

"It's in the closet, under the floorboards. And I need it. I can't go to sleep without my diary." Elena didn't know why she was making such a fuss, but it seemed important.

Damon looked exasperated; then, his face cleared. "Here," he said calmly, eyes glinting. He withdrew something from his jacket. "Take it."

Elena eyed his offering doubtfully.

"It's your diary, isn't it?"

"Yes, but it's my old one. I want my new one."

"This one will have to do, because this one is all you're getting. Come on before they wake up the whole neighborhood." His voice had turned cold and commanding again.

Elena considered the book he held. It was small, with a blue velvet cover and a brass lock. Not the newest edition perhaps, but it was familiar to her. She decided it was acceptable.

She let Damon lead her out into the night.

She didn't ask where they were going. She didn't much care. But she recognized the house on Magnolia Avenue; it was where Alaric Saltzman was staying.

And it was Alaric who opened the front door, beckoning Elena and Damon inside. The history teacher looked strange, though, and didn't really seem to see them. His eyes were glassy and he moved like an automaton.

Elena licked her lips.

"No," Damon said shortly. "This one's not for biting. There's something fishy about him, but you should be safe enough in the house. I've slept here before. Up here." He led her up a flight of stairs to an attic with one small window. It was crowded with stored objects: sleds, skis, a hammock. At the far end, an old mattress lay on the floor.

"He won't even know you're here in the morning. Lie down." Elena obeyed, assuming a position that seemed natural to her. She lay on her back, hands folded over the diary that she held to her breast.

Damon dropped a piece of oilcloth over her, covering her bare feet.

"Go to sleep, Elena," he said.

He bent over her, and for a moment she thought he was going to . . . do something. Her thoughts were too muddled. But his night black eyes filled her vision. Then he pulled back, and she could breathe again. The gloom of the attic settled in on her. Her eyes drifted shut and she slept.

She woke slowly, assembling information about where she was, piece by piece. Somebody's attic from the looks of it. What was she doing here?

Rats or mice were scuffling somewhere among the piles of oilcloth-draped objects, but the sound didn't bother her. The faintest trace of pale light showed around the edges of the shuttered window. Elena pushed her makeshift blanket off and got up to investigate.

It was definitely someone's attic, and not that of anyone she knew. She felt as if she had been sick for a long time and had just woken up from her illness. What day is it? she wondered.

She could hear voices below her. Downstairs. Something told her to be careful and quiet. She felt afraid of making any kind of disturbance. She eased the attic door open without a sound and cautiously descended to the landing. Looking down, she could see a living room. She recognized it; she'd sat on that ottoman when Alaric Saltzman had given a party. She was in the Ramsey house.

And Alaric Saltzman was down there; she could see the top of his sandy head. His voice puzzled her. After a moment she realized it was because he didn't sound fatuous or inane or any of the ways Alaric usually sounded in class. He wasn't spouting psycho-babble, either. He was speaking coolly and decisively to two other men.

"She might be anywhere, even right under our noses. More likely outside town, though. Maybe in the woods."

"Why the woods?" said one of the men. Elena knew that voice, too, and that bald head. It was Mr. Newcastle, the high school principal.

"Remember, the first two victims were found near the woods," said the other man. Is

51

that Dr. Feinberg? Elena thought. What's he doing here? What am *I* doing here?

"No, it's more than that," Alaric was saying. The other men were listening to him with respect, even with deference. "The woods are tied up in this. They may have a hiding place out there, a lair where they can go to earth if they're discovered. If there is one, I'll find it."

"Are you sure?" said Dr. Feinberg.

"I'm sure," Alaric said briefly.

"And that's where you think Elena is," said the principal. "But will she stay there? Or will she come back into town?"

"I don't know." Alaric paced a few steps and picked up a book from the coffee table, running his thumbs over it absently. "One way to find out is to watch her friends. Bonnie McCullough and that dark-haired girl, Meredith. Chances are they'll be the first ones to see her. That's how it usually happens."

"And once we do track her down?" Dr. Feinberg asked.

"Leave that to me," Alaric said quietly and grimly. He shut the book and dropped it on the coffee table with a disturbingly conclusive sound.

The principal glanced at his watch. "I'd

better get moving; the service starts at ten o'clock. I presume you'll both be there?" He paused on his way to the door and looked back, his manner irresolute. "Alaric, I hope you can take care of this. When I called you in, things hadn't gone this far. Now I'm beginning to wonder—"

"I *can* take care of it, Brian. I told you; leave it to me. Would you rather have Robert E. Lee in all the papers, not just as the scene of a tragedy but also as 'The Haunted High School of Boone County'? A gathering place for ghouls? The school where the undead walk? Is that the kind of publicity you want?"

Mr. Newcastle hesitated, chewing his lip, then nodded, still looking unhappy. "All right, Alaric. But make it quick and clean. I'll see you at the church." He left and Dr. Feinberg followed him.

Alaric stood there for some time, apparently staring into space. At last he nodded once and went out the front door himself.

Elena slowly trailed back up the stairs.

Now what had all that been about? She felt confused, as if she were floating loose in time and space. She needed to know what day it was, why she was here, and why she felt so frightened. Why she felt so intensely that no

sat as still as she could get. What caused the panic was that she *remembered*.

She remembered everything now.

The bridge, the rushing water. The terror as the air left her lungs and there was nothing but liquid to breathe. The way it had hurt. And the final instant when it had stopped hurting, when everything had stopped. When everything . . . stopped.

Oh, Stefan, I was so frightened, she thought. And the same fear was inside her now. In the woods, how could she have behaved like that to Stefan? How could she have forgotten him, everything he meant to her? What had made her act that way?

But she knew. At the center of her consciousness, she knew. Nobody got up and walked away from a drowning like that. Nobody got up and walked away alive.

Slowly, she rose and went to look at the shuttered window. The darkened pane of glass acted as a mirror, throwing her reflection back at her.

It was not the reflection she'd seen in her dream, where she had run down a hall of mirrors that seemed to have a life of their own. There was nothing sly or cruel about this face. Just the same, it was subtly different from what she was used to seeing. There was a pale glow to her skin and a telling hollowness about the eyes. Elena touched fingertips to her neck, on either side. This was where Stefan and Damon had each taken her blood. Had it really been enough times, and had she really taken enough of theirs in return?

It must have been. And now, for the rest of her life, for the rest of her existence, she would have to feed as Stefan did. She would have to . . .

She sank to her knees, pressing her forehead against the bare wood of a wall. I can't, she thought. Oh, please, I can't; I can't.

She had never been very religious. But from that deep place inside, her terror was welling up, and every particle of her being joined in the cry for aid. Oh, please, she thought. Oh, please, please, help me. She didn't ask for anything specific; she couldn't gather her thoughts that far. Only: Oh, please help me, oh please, *please*.

After a while she got up again.

Her face was still pale but eerily beautiful, like fine porcelain lit from within. Her eyes were still smudged with shadows. But there was a resolve in them.

She had to find Stefan. If there was any

help for her, he would know of it. And if there wasn't . . . well, she needed him all the more. There was nowhere else she wanted to be except with him.

She shut the door of the attic carefully behind her as she went out. Alaric Saltzman mustn't discover her hiding place. On the wall, she saw a calendar with the days up to December 4 crossed off. Four days since last Saturday night. She'd slept for four days.

When she reached the front door, she cringed from the daylight outside. It hurt. Even though the sky was so overcast that rain or snow looked imminent, it hurt her eyes. She had to force herself to leave the safety of the house, and then she felt a gnawing paranoia about being out in the open. She slunk along beside fences, staying close to trees, ready to melt into the shadows. She felt like a shadow herself—or a ghost, in Honoria Fell's long white gown. She would frighten the wits out of anyone who saw her.

But all her circumspection seemed to be wasted. There was no one on the streets to see her; the town might have been abandoned. She went by seemingly deserted houses, forsaken yards, closed stores. Presently she saw parked cars lining the street, but they were empty, too.

And then she saw a shape against the sky that stopped her in her tracks. A steeple, white against the thick dark clouds. Elena's legs trembled as she made herself creep closer to the building. She'd known this church all her life; she'd seen the cross inscribed on that wall a thousand times. But now she edged toward it as if it were a caged animal that might break loose and bite her. She pressed one hand to the stone wall and slid it nearer and nearer to the carved symbol.

When her outspread fingers touched the arm of the cross, her eyes filled and her throat ached. She let her hand glide along it until it gently covered the engraving. Then she leaned against the wall and let the tears come.

I'm not evil, she thought. I did things I shouldn't have. I thought about myself too much; I never thanked Matt and Bonnie and Meredith for all they did for me. I should have played more with Margaret and been nicer to Aunt Judith. But I'm not evil. I'm not damned.

When she could see again, she looked up at the building. Mr. Newcastle had said something about the church. Was it this one he meant?

She avoided the front of the church and the main doorway. There was a side door that led to the choir loft, and she slipped up the stairs noiselessly and looked down from the gallery.

She saw at once why the streets had been so empty. It seemed as if everyone in Fell's Church was here, every seat in every pew filled, and the back of the church packed solid with people standing. Staring at the front rows, Elena realized that she recognized every face; they were members of the senior class, and neighbors, and friends of Aunt Judith. Aunt Judith was there, too, wearing the black dress she'd worn to Elena's parents' funeral.

Oh, my God, Elena thought. Her fingers gripped the railing. Until now she'd been too busy looking to listen, but the quiet monotone of Reverend Bethea's voice suddenly resolved into words.

". . . share our remembrances of this very special girl," he said, and he moved aside.

Elena watched what happened after with the unearthly feeling that she had a loge seat at a play. She was not at all involved in the events down there on stage; she was only a spectator, but it was *her* life she was watching.

Mr. Carson, Sue Carson's father, came up and talked about her. The Carsons had known her since she was born, and he talked about the days she and Sue had played in their front yard in the summer. He talked about the beautiful and accomplished young lady she had become. He got a frog in his throat and had to stop and take off his glasses.

Sue Carson went up. She and Elena hadn't been close friends since elementary school, but they'd remained on good terms. Sue had been one of the few girls who'd stayed on Elena's side after Stefan had come under suspicion for Mr. Tanner's murder. But now Sue was crying as if she'd lost a sister.

"A lot of people weren't nice to Elena after Halloween," she said, wiping her eyes and going on. "And I know that hurt her. But Elena was *strong*. She never changed just to conform to what other people thought she should be. And I respected her for that, so much . . ." Sue's voice wobbled. "When I was up for Homecoming Queen, I wanted to be chosen, but I knew I wouldn't be and that was all right. Because if Robert E. Lee ever had a queen, it was Elena. And I think she always will be now, because that's how we'll all remember her. And I think that for years to come the girls who will go to our school might remember her and think about how she stuck by what she thought was right. . . ." This time Sue couldn't steady her voice and the reverend helped her back to her seat.

The girls in the senior class, even the ones that had been nastiest and most spiteful, were crying and holding hands. Girls Elena knew for a fact hated her were sniffling. Suddenly she was everybody's best friend.

There were boys crying, too. Shocked, Elena huddled closer to the railing. She couldn't stop watching, even though it was the most horrible thing she had ever seen.

Frances Decatur got up, her plain face plainer than ever with grief. "She went out of her way to be nice to me," she said huskily. "She let me eat lunch with her." Rubbish, Elena thought. I only spoke to you in the first place because you were useful in finding out information about Stefan. But it was the same with each person who went up to the pulpit; no one could find enough words to praise Elena.

"I always admired her. . . ."

"She was a role model to me. . . ."

"One of my favorite students . . ."

When Meredith rose, Elena's whole body stiffened. She didn't know if she could deal with this. But the dark-haired girl was one of the few people in the church who wasn't crying, although her face had a grave, sad look that reminded Elena of Honoria Fell as she looked on her tomb.

"When I think about Elena, I think about the good times we had together," she said, speaking quietly and with her customary self-control. "Elena always had ideas, and she could make the most boring work into fun. I never told her that, and now I wish I had. I wish that I could talk to her one more time, just so she would know. And if Elena could hear me now"—Meredith looked around the church and drew a long breath, apparently to calm herself—"if she could hear me now, I would tell her how much those good times meant to me, and how much I wish that we could still have them. Like the Thursday nights we used to sit together in her room, practicing for the debate team. I wish we could do that just once more like we used to."

Meredith took another long breath and

shook her head. "But I know we can't, and that hurts."

What are you talking about? Elena thought, her misery interrupted by bewilderment. We used to practice for the debate team on *Wednesday* nights, not Thursdays. And it wasn't in my bedroom; it was in yours. And it was no fun at all; in fact, we ended up quitting because we both hated it. . . .

Suddenly, watching Meredith's carefully composed face, so calm on the outside to conceal the tension within, Elena felt her heart begin to pound.

Meredith was sending a message, a message only Elena could be expected to understand. Which meant that Meredith expected Elena to be able to hear it.

Meredith knew.

Had Stefan told her? Elena scanned the rows of mourners below, realizing for the first time that Stefan wasn't among them. Neither was Matt. No, it didn't seem likely that Stefan would have told Meredith, or that Meredith would choose this way of getting a message to her If he had. Then Elena remembered the way Meredith had looked at her the night they had rescued Stefan from the well, when Elena had asked to be left alone with Stefan.

She remembered those keen dark eyes studying her face more than once in the last months, and the way Meredith had seemed to grow quieter and more thoughtful each time Elena came up with some odd request.

Meredith had guessed then. Elena wondered just how much of the truth she'd put together.

Bonnie was coming up now, crying in earnest. That was surprising; if Meredith knew, why hadn't she told Bonnie? But maybe Meredith had only a suspicion, something she didn't want to share with Bonnie in case it turned out to be a false hope.

Bonnie's speech was as emotional as Meredith's had been collected. Her voice kept breaking and she kept having to brush tears off her cheeks. Finally Reverend Bethea crossed over and gave her something white, a handkerchief or some tissue.

"Thank you," Bonnie said, wiping her streaming eyes. She tilted her head back to look at the ceiling, either to regain her poise or to get inspiration. As she did, Elena saw something that no one else could see: she saw Bonnie's face drain of color and of expression, not like somebody about to faint, but in a way that was all too familiar.

A chill crawled up Elena's backbone. Not here. Oh, God, of all times and places, not here.

But it was already happening. Bonnie's chin had lowered; she was looking at the congregation again. Except that this time she didn't seem to see them at all, and the voice that came from Bonnie's throat was not Bonnie's voice.

"No one is what they appear. Remember that. *No one is what they appear.*" Then she just stood there, unmoving, staring straight ahead with blank eyes.

People began to shuffle and look at one another. There was a murmur of worry.

"Remember that—remember—no one is what they seem . . ." Bonnie swayed suddenly, and Reverend Bethea ran to her while another man hastened up from the other side. The second man had a bald head that was now shining with sweat—Mr. Newcastle, Elena realized. And there at the back of the church, striding up the nave, was Alaric Saltzman. He reached Bonnie just as she fainted, and Elena heard a step behind her on the stair.

Five

Dr. Feinberg, Elena thought wildly, trying to twist around to look and simultaneously press herself into the shadows. But it wasn't the small, hawk-nosed visage of the doctor that met her eyes. It was a face with features as fine as those on a Roman coin or medallion, and haunted green eyes. Time caught for a moment, and then Elena was in his arms.

"Oh, Stefan. Stefan . . ."

She felt his body go still with shock. He was holding her mechanically, lightly, as if she were a stranger who'd mistaken him for someone else.

"*Stefan*," she said desperately, burrowing her face into his shoulder, trying to get some response. She couldn't bear it if he rejected her; if he hated her now she would *die*. . . .

With a moan, she tried to get even closer to him, wanting to merge with him completely, to disappear inside him. Oh, please, she thought, oh, please, oh, please. . . .

"Elena. Elena, it's all right; I've got you." He went on talking to her, repeating silly nonsense meant to soothe, stroking her hair. And she could feel the change as his arms tightened around her. He knew who he was holding now. For the first time since she'd awakened that day, she felt safe. Still, it was a long while before she could relax her grip on him even slightly. She wasn't crying; she was gasping in panic.

At last she felt the world start to settle into place around her. She didn't let go, though, not yet. She simply stood for endless minutes with her head on his shoulder, drinking in the comfort and security of his nearness.

Then she raised her head to look into his eyes.

When she'd thought of Stefan earlier that day, she'd thought of how he might help her. She'd meant to ask him, to beg him, to save her from this nightmare, to make her the way she had been before. But now, as she looked at him, she felt a strange despairing resignation flow through her.

"There's nothing to be done about it, is there?" she said very softly.

He didn't pretend to misunderstand. "No," he said, equally soft.

Elena felt as if she had taken some final step over an invisible line and that there was no returning. When she could speak again, she said, "I'm sorry for the way I acted toward you in the woods. I don't know why I did those things. I remember doing them, but I can't remember *why*."

"*You're* sorry?" His voice shook. "Elena, after all I've done to you, all that's happened to you because of me . . ." He couldn't finish, and they clung to each other.

"Very touching," said a voice from the stairway. "Do you want me to imitate a violin?"

Elena's calm shattered, and fear snaked through her bloodstream. She'd forgotten Damon's hypnotic intensity and his burning dark eyes.

"How did you get here?" said Stefan.

"The same way you did, I presume. Attracted by the blazing beacon of the fair Elena's distress." Damon was really angry;

Elena could tell. Not just annoyed or discommoded but in a white heat of rage and hostility.

But he'd been decent to her when she'd been confused and irrational. He'd taken her to shelter; he'd kept her safe. And he hadn't kissed her while she'd been in that horrifyingly vulnerable state. He'd been . . . kind to her.

"Incidentally, there's something going on down there," Damon said.

"I know; it's Bonnie again," said Elena, releasing Stefan and moving back.

"That's not what I meant. This is outside."

Startled, Elena followed him down to the first bend in the stairs, where there was a window overlooking the parking lot. She felt Stefan behind her as she looked down at the scene below.

A crowd of people had come out of the church, but they were standing in a solid phalanx at the edge of the lot, not going any farther. Opposite them, in the parking lot itself, was an equally large assembly of dogs.

It looked like two armies facing each other. What was eerie, though, was that both groups were absolutely motionless. The people seemed to be paralyzed by uneasiness, and the dogs seemed to be waiting for something.

Elena saw the dogs first as different breeds. There were small dogs like sharp-faced corgis and brown-and-black silky terriers and a Lhasa apso with long golden hair. There were medium-sized dogs like springer spaniels and Airedales and one beautiful snow white Samoyed. And there were the big dogs: a barrel-chested rottweiler with a cropped tail, a panting gray wolfhound, and a giant schnauzer, pure black. Then Elena began to recognize individuals.

"That's Mr. Grunbaum's boxer and the Sullivans' German shepherd. But what's going on with them?"

The people, originally uneasy, now looked frightened. They stood shoulder to shoulder, no one wanting to break out of the front line and move any closer to the animals.

And yet the dogs weren't *doing* anything, just sitting or standing, some with their tongues lolling gently out. Strange, though, how still they were, Elena thought. Every tiny motion, such as the slightest twitch of tail or ears, seemed vastly exaggerated. And there were no wagging tails, no signs of friendliness. Just . . . waiting.

Robert was toward the back of the crowd. Elena was surprised at seeing him, but for a moment she couldn't think of why. Then she realized it was because he hadn't been in the church. As she watched, he drew farther apart from the group, disappearing under the overhang below Elena.

"Chelsea! Chelsea . . ."

Someone had moved out of the front line at last. It was Douglas Carson, Elena realized, Sue Carson's married older brother. He'd stepped into the no-man's-land between the dogs and the people, one hand slightly extended.

A springer spaniel with long ears like brown satin turned her head. Her white stump of a tail quivered slightly, questioningly, and her brown-and-white muzzle lifted. But she didn't come to the young man.

Doug Carson took another step. "Chelsea . . . good girl. Come here, Chelsea. Come!" He snapped his fingers.

"What do you sense from those dogs down there?" Damon murmured.

Stefan shook his head without looking away from the window. "Nothing," he said shortly.

"Neither do I." Damon's eyes were narrowed, his head tilted back appraisingly, but his slightly bared teeth reminded Elena of the wolfhound. "But we *should* be able to, you know. They ought to have some emotions we can pick up on. Instead, every time I try to probe them it's like running into a blank white wall."

Elena wished she knew what they were talking about. "What do you mean 'probe them'?" she said. "They're animals."

"Appearances can be deceiving," Damon said ironically, and Elena thought about the rainbow lights in the feathers of the crow that had followed her since the first day of school. If she looked closely, she could see those same rainbow lights in Damon's silky hair. "But animals have emotions, in any case. If your Powers are strong enough, you can examine their minds."

And my Powers aren't, thought Elena. She was startled by the twinge of envy that went through her. Just a few minutes ago she'd been clinging to Stefan, frantic to get rid of any Powers she had, to change herself *back*. And now, she wished she were stronger. Damon always had an odd effect on her.

"I may not be able to probe Chelsea, but I

don't think Doug should go any closer," she said aloud.

Stefan had been staring fixedly out the window, his eyebrows drawn together. Now he nodded fractionally, but with a sudden sense of urgency. "I don't either," he said.

"C'mon, Chelsea, be a good girl. Come here." Doug Carson had almost reached the first row of dogs. All eyes, human and canine, were fixed on him, and even such tiny movements as twitches had stopped. If Elena hadn't seen the sides of one or two dogs hollow and fill with their breathing, she might have thought the whole group was some giant museum display.

Doug had come to a halt. Chelsea was watching him from behind the corgi and the Samoyed. Doug clucked his tongue. He stretched out his hand, hesitated, and then stretched it out farther.

"No," Elena said. She was staring at the rottweiler's glossy flanks. Hollow and fill, hollow and fill. "Stefan, influence him. Get him out of there."

"Yes." She could see his gaze unfocus with concentration; then, he shook his head, exhaling like a person who's tried to lift something too heavy. "It's no good; I'm burnt out. I can't do it from here."

Below, Chelsea's lips skinned back from her teeth. The red-gold Airedale rose to her feet in one beautifully smooth movement, as if pulled by strings. The hindquarters of the rottweiler bunched.

And then they sprang. Elena couldn't see which of the dogs was the first; they seemed to move together like a great wave. Half a dozen hit Doug Carson with enough force to knock him backward, and he disappeared under their massed bodies.

The air was full of hellish noise, from a metallic baying that set the church rafters ringing and gave Elena an instant headache, to a deep-throated continuous growl that she felt rather than heard. Dogs were tearing at clothing, snarling, lunging, while the crowd scattered and screamed.

Elena caught sight of Alaric Saltzman at the edge of the parking lot, the only one who wasn't running. He was standing stiffly, and she thought she could see his lips moving, and his hands.

Everywhere else was pandemonium. Someone had gotten a hose and was turning it into the thick of the pack, but it was having no effect. The dogs seemed to have gone mad. When Chelsea raised her brown-and-white muzzle from her master's body, it was tinged with red.

Elena's heart was pounding so that she could barely breathe. "They need help!" she said, just as Stefan broke away from the window and went down the stairs, taking them two and three at a time. Elena was halfway down the stairs herself when she realized two things: Damon wasn't following her, and she couldn't let herself be seen.

She *couldn't*. The hysteria it would cause, the questions, the fear and hatred once the questions were answered. Something that ran deeper than compassion or sympathy or the need to help wrenched her back, flattening her against the wall.

In the dim, cool interior of the church, she glimpsed a boiling pocket of activity. People were dashing back and forth, shouting. Dr. Feinberg, Mr. McCullough, Reverend Bethea. The still point of the circle was Bonnie lying on a pew with Meredith and Aunt Judith and Mrs. McCullough bent over her. "Something evil," she was moaning, and then Aunt Judith's head came up, turning in Elena's direction.

Elena scuttled up the stairs as quickly as she could, praying Aunt Judith hadn't seen her. Damon was at the window.

"I can't go down there. They think I'm dead!"

"Oh, you've remembered that. Good for you."

"If Dr. Feinberg examines me, he'll know something's wrong. Well, won't he?" she demanded fiercely.

"He'll think you're an interesting specimen, all right."

"Then I can't go. But you can. Why don't you *do* something?"

Damon continued to look out the window, eyebrows hiking up. "Why?"

"Why?" Elena's alarm and overexcitement reached flash point and she almost slapped him. "Because they need help! Because you *can* help. Don't you care about anything besides yourself?"

Damon was wearing his most impenetrable mask, the expression of polite inquiry he'd worn when he invited himself to her house for dinner. But she knew that beneath it he was angry, angry at finding her and Stefan together. He was baiting her on purpose and with savage enjoyment.

one must see her or hear her or notice her at all.

Looking around the attic, she saw nothing that would give her any help. Where she had been lying there were only the mattress and the oilcloth—and a little blue book.

Her diary! Eagerly, she snatched it up and opened it, skipping through the entries. They stopped with October 17; they were no help to discovering today's date. But as she looked at the writing, images formed in her mind, stringing up like pearls to make memories. Fascinated, she slowly sat down on the mattress. She leafed back to the beginning and began to read about the life of Elena Gilbert.

When she finished, she was weak with fear and horror. Bright spots danced and shimmered before her eyes. There was so much pain in these pages. So many schemes, so many secrets, so much need. It was the story of a girl who'd felt lost in her own hometown, in her own family. Who'd been looking for . . . something, something she could never quite reach. But that wasn't what caused this throbbing panic in her chest that drained all the energy from her body. That wasn't why she felt as if she were falling even when she were much more powerful than the garden hose, and the jet streams of water drove the lunging dogs off with sheer force. Elena saw a sheriff with a gun and bit the inside of her cheek as he aimed and sighted. There was a crack, and the giant schnauzer went down. The sheriff aimed again.

It ended quickly after that. Several dogs were already running from the barrage of water, and with the second crack of the pistol more broke from the pack and headed for the edges of the parking lot. It was as if the purpose that had driven them had released them all at once. Elena felt a rush of relief as she saw Stefan standing unharmed in the middle of the rout, shoving a dazed-looking golden retriever away from Doug Carson's form. Chelsea took a skulking step toward her master and looked into his face, head and tail drooping.

"It's all over," Damon said. He sounded only mildly interested, but Elena glanced at him sharply. All right then, damn you, I'll *what*? she thought. What had he been about to say? He wasn't in any mood to tell her, but she was in a mood to push.

"Damon . . ." She put a hand on his arm. He stiffened, then turned. "Well?"

For a second they stood looking at each other, and then there was a step on the stair. Stefan had returned.

"Stefan . . . you're hurt," she said, blinking, suddenly disoriented.

"I'm all right." He wiped blood off his cheek with a tattered sleeve.

"What about Doug?" Elena asked, swallowing.

"I don't know. He *is* hurt. A lot of people are. That was the strangest thing I've ever seen."

Elena moved away from Damon, up the stairs into the choir loft. She felt that she had to think, but her head was pounding. The strangest thing Stefan had ever seen . . . that was saying a lot. Something strange in Fell's Church.

She reached the wall behind the last row of seats and put a hand against it, sliding down to sit on the floor. Things seemed at once confused and frighteningly clear. Something strange in Fell's Church. The day of the founders' celebration she would have sworn she didn't care anything about Fell's Church or the people in it. But now she knew differently. Looking down on the memorial service, she had begun to think perhaps she *did* care.

And then, when the dogs had attacked outside, she'd known it. She felt somehow responsible for the town, in a way she had never felt before.

Her earlier sense of desolation and loneliness had been pushed aside for the moment. There was something more important than her own problems now. And she clung to that something, because the truth was that she really couldn't deal with her own situation, no, she really, really couldn't. . . .

She heard the gasping half sob she gave then and looked up to see both Stefan and Damon in the choir loft, looking at her. She shook her head slightly, putting a hand to it, feeling as if she were coming out of a dream.

"Elena . . . ?"

It was Stefan who spoke, but Elena addressed herself to the other one.

"Damon," she said shakily, "if I ask you something, will you tell me the truth? I know you didn't chase me off Wickery Bridge. I could *feel* whatever it was, and it was different. But I want to ask you this: was it you who dumped Stefan in the old Francher well a month ago?"

"In a *well?*" Damon leaned back against the

opposite wall, arms crossed over his chest. He looked politely incredulous.

"On Halloween night, the night Mr. Tanner was killed. After you showed yourself for the first time to Stefan in the woods. He told me he left you in the clearing and started to walk to his car but that someone attacked him before he reached it. When he woke up, he was trapped in the well, and he would have died there if Bonnie hadn't led us to him. I always assumed you were the one who attacked him. *He* always assumed you were the one. But were you?"

Damon's lip curled, as if he didn't like the demanding intensity of her question. He looked from her to Stefan with hooded, deriding eyes. The moment stretched out until Elena had to dig her fingernails into her palms with tension. Then Damon gave a small shrug and looked off at a middle distance.

"As a matter of fact, no," he said.

Elena let out her breath.

"You can't believe that!" Stefan exploded. "You can't believe anything he says."

"Why should I lie?" Damon returned, clearly enjoying Stefan's loss of control. "I admit freely to killing Tanner. I drank his blood

82

until he shriveled like a prune. And I wouldn't mind doing the same thing to *you*, brother. But a *well*? It's hardly my style."

"I believe you," Elena said. Her mind was rushing ahead. She turned to Stefan. "Don't you feel it? There's something else here in Fell's Church, something that may not even be human—may never have been human, I mean. Something that chased me, forced my car off the bridge. Something that made those dogs attack people. Some terrible force that's here, something evil . . ." Her voice trailed off, and she looked over toward the interior of the church where she had seen Bonnie lying. "Something evil . . ." she repeated softly. A cold wind seemed to blow inside her, and she huddled into herself, feeling vulnerable and alone.

"If you're looking for evil," Stefan said harshly, "you don't have to look far."

"Don't be any more stupid than you can help," said Damon. "I told you four days ago that someone else had killed Elena. And I said that I was going to find that someone and deal with him. And I am." He uncrossed his arms and straightened up. "You two can continue that private conversation you were having when I interrupted."

"Damon, wait." Elena hadn't been able to help the shudder that tore through her when he said *killed*. I can't have been killed; I'm still here, she thought wildly, feeling panic swell up in her again. But now she pushed the panic aside to speak to Damon.

"Whatever this thing is, it's strong," she said. "I felt it when it was after me, and it seemed to fill the whole sky. I don't think any of us would stand a chance against it alone."

"So?"

"So . . ." Elena hadn't had time to gather her thoughts this far. She was running purely on instinct, on intuition. And intuition told her not to let Damon go. "So . . . I think we three ought to stick together. I think we have a much better chance of finding it and dealing with it together than separately. And maybe we can stop it before it hurts or—or kills—anyone else."

"Frankly, my dear, I don't give a damn about anyone else," Damon said charmingly. Then he gave one of his ice-cold lightning smiles. "But are you suggesting that this is your choice? Remember, we agreed that when you were more rational you would make one."

Elena stared at him. Of course it wasn't her

choice, if he meant romantically. She was wearing the ring Stefan had given her; she and Stefan belonged together.

But then she remembered something else, just a flash: looking up at Damon's face in the woods and feeling such—such excitement, such affinity with him. As if he understood the flame that burned inside her as nobody else ever could. As if together they could do anything they liked, conquer the world or destroy it; as if they were better than anyone else who had ever lived.

I was out of my mind, irrational, she told herself, but that little flash of memory wouldn't go away.

And then she remembered something else: how Damon had acted later that night, how he'd kept her safe, even been gentle with her.

Stefan was looking at her, and his expression had changed from belligerence to bitter anger and fear. Part of her wanted to reassure him completely, to throw her arms around him and tell him that she was his and always would be and that nothing else mattered. Not the town, not Damon, not anything.

But she wasn't doing it. Because another part of her was saying that the town *did* matter. And because still another part was just terribly, terribly confused. So confused . . .

She felt a trembling begin deep inside her, and then she found she couldn't make it stop. Emotional overload, she thought, and put her head in her hands.

Six

"She's already made her choice. You saw it yourself when you 'interrupted' us. You've already chosen, haven't you, Elena?" Stefan said it not smugly, or as a demand, but with a kind of desperate bravado.

"I . . ." Elena looked up. "Stefan, I love you. But don't you understand, if I have a choice right now I have to choose for all of us to stay together. Just for now. *Do* you understand?" Seeing only stoniness in Stefan's face, she turned to Damon. "Do you?"

"I think so." He gave her a secret, possessive smile. "I told Stefan from the beginning that he was selfish not to share you. Brothers should share things, you know."

"That's not what I meant."

"Isn't it?" Damon smiled again.

"No," Stefan said. "*I* don't understand, and I don't see how you can ask me to work with *him*. He's evil, Elena. He kills for pleasure; he has no conscience at all. He doesn't care about Fell's Church; he said that himself. He's a monster—"

"Right now he's being more cooperative than you are," Elena said. She reached for Stefan's hand, searching for some way to get through to him. "Stefan, I *need* you. And we both need him. Can't you try to accept that?" When he didn't answer she added, "Stefan, do you really want to be mortal enemies with your brother forever?"

"Do you really think *he* wants anything else?"

Elena stared down at their joined hands, looking at the planes and curves and shadows. She didn't answer for a minute, and when she did it was very quietly.

"He stopped me from killing you," she said.

She felt the flare of Stefan's defensive anger, then felt it slowly fade. Something like defeat crept through him, and he bowed his head.

"That's true," he said. "And, anyway, who

am I to call him evil? What's he done that I haven't done myself?"

We need to talk, Elena thought, hating this self-hatred of his. But this wasn't the time or place.

"Then you do agree?" she said hesitantly. "Stefan, tell me what you're thinking."

"Right now I'm thinking that you always get your way. Because you always do, don't you, Elena?"

Elena looked into his eyes, noticing how the pupils were dilated, so that only a ring of green iris showed around the edge. There was no longer anger there, but the tiredness and the bitterness remained.

But I'm not just doing it for myself, she thought, thrusting out of her mind the sudden surge of self-doubt. I'll prove that to you, Stefan; you'll see. For once I'm not doing something for my own convenience.

"Then you agree?" she said quietly.

"Yes. I . . . agree."

"And *I* agree," said Damon, extending his own hand with exaggerated courtesy. He captured Elena's before she could say anything. "In fact, we all seem to be in a frenzy of pure agreement."

Don't, Elena thought, but at that moment,

standing in the cool twilight of the choir loft, she felt that it was true, that they were all three connected, and in accord, and strong.

Then Stefan pulled his hand away. In the silence that followed, Elena could hear the sounds outside and in the church below. There was still crying and the occasional shout, but the overall urgency was gone. Looking out the window, she saw people picking their way across the wet parking lot between the little groups that huddled over wounded victims. Dr. Feinberg was moving from island to island, apparently dispensing medical advice. The victims looked like survivors of a hurricane or earthquake.

"No one is what they seem," Elena said.

"What?"

"That's what Bonnie said during the memorial service. She had another one of her fits. I think it might be important." She tried to put her thoughts in order. "I think there are people in town that we ought to look out for. Like Alaric Saltzman." She told them, briefly, what she had overheard earlier that day in Alaric's house. "*He's* not what he seems, but I don't know exactly what he is. I think we should watch him. And since I obviously can't appear in public, you two are going to have to do it. But you can't let him suspect you know—" Elena broke off as Damon held up a hand swiftly.

Down at the base of the stairs, a voice was calling. "Stefan? Are you up there?" And then, to someone else, "I thought I saw him go up here."

It sounded like Mr. Carson. "Go," Elena hissed almost inaudibly to Stefan. "You have to be as normal as possible so you can stay here in Fell's Church. I'll be all right."

"But where will *you* go?"

"To Meredith's. I'll explain later. Go on."

Stefan hesitated, and then started down the stairs, calling, "I'm coming." Then he pulled back. "I'm not leaving you with *him*," he said flatly.

Elena threw her hands up in exasperation. "Then both of you go. You just agreed to work together; are you going to go back on your word now?" she added to Damon, who was looking unyielding himself.

He gave another of his little shrugs. "All right. Just one thing—are you hungry?"

"I—no." Stomach lurching, Elena realized what he was asking. "No, not at all."

"That's good. But later on, you will be. Remember that." He crowded Stefan down the stairs, earning himself a searing look. But Elena heard Stefan's voice in her mind as they both disappeared.

I'll come for you later. Wait for me.

She wished she could answer with her own thoughts. She also noticed something. Stefan's mental voice was much weaker than it had been four days ago when he had been fighting his brother. Come to think of it, he hadn't been able to speak with his mind at all before the Founders' Day celebration. She'd been so confused when she woke up by the river that it hadn't occurred to her, but now she wondered. What had happened to make him so strong? And why was his strength fading now?

Elena had time to think about it as she sat there in the deserted choir loft, while below the people left the church and outside the overcast skies slowly grew darker. She thought about Stefan, and about Damon, and she wondered if she had made the right choice. She'd vowed never to let them fight over her, but that vow was broken already. Was she crazy to try and make them live under a truce, even a temporary one?

When the sky outside was uniformly black, she ventured down the stairs. The church was empty and echoing. She hadn't thought about how she would get out, but fortunately the side door was bolted only from the inside. She slipped out into the night gratefully.

She hadn't realized how good it was to be outside and in the dark. Being inside buildings made her feel trapped, and daylight hurt her eyes. This was best, free and unfettered—and unseen. Her own senses rejoiced at the lush world around her. With the air so still, scents hung in the air for a long time, and she could smell a whole plethora of nocturnal creatures. A fox was scavenging in somebody's trash. Brown rats were chewing something in the bushes. Night moths were calling to one another with scent.

She found it wasn't hard to get to Meredith's house undetected; people seemed to be staying inside. But once she got there, she stood looking up at the graceful farmhouse with the screened porch in dismay. She couldn't just walk up to the front door and knock. Was Meredith really expecting her? Wouldn't she be waiting outside if she were?

Meredith was about to get a terrible shock if she *weren't*, Elena reflected, eyeing the distance to the roof of the porch. Meredith's bedroom window was above it and just around the corner. It would be a bit of a reach, but Elena thought she could make it.

Getting onto the roof was easy; her fingers and bare toes found holds between the bricks and sent her sailing up. But leaning around the corner to look into Meredith's window was a strain. She blinked against the light that flooded out.

Meredith was sitting on the edge of her bed, elbows on knees, staring at nothing. Every so often she ran a hand through her dark hair. A clock on the nightstand said 6:43.

Elena tapped on the window glass with her fingernails.

Meredith jumped and looked the wrong way, toward the door. She stood up in a defensive crouch, clutching a throw pillow in one hand. When the door didn't open, she sidled a pace or two toward it, still in a defensive posture. "Who is it?" she said.

Elena tapped on the glass again.

Meredith spun to face the window, her breath coming fast.

"Let me in," said Elena. She didn't know if Meredith could hear her, so she mouthed it clearly. "Open the window."

Meredith, panting, looked around the room as if she expected someone to appear and help her. When no one did, she approached the window as if it were a dangerous animal. But she didn't open it.

"Let me *in*," Elena said again. Then she added impatiently, "If you didn't want me to come, why did you make an appointment with me?"

She saw the change as Meredith's shoulders relaxed slightly. Slowly, with fingers that were unusually clumsy, Meredith opened the window and stood back.

"Now ask me to come inside. Otherwise I can't."

"Come . . ." Meredith's voice failed and she had to try again. "Come in," she said. When Elena, wincing, had boosted herself over the sill and was flexing her cramped fingers, Meredith added almost dazedly, "It's got to be you. Nobody else gives orders like that."

"It's me," Elena said. She stopped wringing out the cramps and looked into the eyes of her friend. "It really is me, Meredith," she said.

Meredith nodded and swallowed visibly. Right then what Elena would have liked most in the world would have been for the other girl to give her a hug. But Meredith wasn't much of the hugging type, and right now she was backing slowly away to sit on the bed again.

"Sit down," she said in an artificially calm voice. Elena pulled out the desk chair and unthinkingly took up the same position Meredith had been in before, elbows on knees, head down. Then she looked up. "How did you know?"

"I . . ." Meredith just stared at her for a moment, then shook herself. "Well. You—your body was never found, of course. That was strange. And then those attacks on the old man and Vickie and Tanner—and Stefan and little things I'd put together about him—but I didn't *know*. Not for sure. Not until now." She ended almost in a whisper.

"Well, it was a good guess," Elena said. She was trying to behave normally, but what was normal in this situation? Meredith was acting as if she could scarcely bear to look at her. It made Elena feel more lonely, more alone, than she could ever remember being in her life.

A doorbell rang downstairs. Elena heard it, but she could tell Meredith didn't. "Who's coming?" she said. "There's someone at the door."

"I asked Bonnie to come over at seven

o'clock, if her mother would let her. It's probably her. I'll go see." Meredith seemed almost indecently eager to get away.

"Wait. Does *she* know?"

"No. . . . Oh, you mean I should break it to her gently." Meredith looked around the room again uncertainly, and Elena snapped on the little reading light by the bed.

"Turn the room light off. It hurts my eyes anyway," she said quietly. When Meredith did, the bedroom was dim enough that she could conceal herself in the shadows.

Waiting for Meredith to return with Bonnie, she stood in a corner, hugging her elbows with her hands. Maybe it was a bad idea trying to get Meredith and Bonnie involved. If imperturbable Meredith couldn't handle the situation, what would Bonnie do?

Meredith heralded their arrival by muttering over and over, "Don't scream now; *don't scream*," as she bundled Bonnie across the threshold.

"What's *wrong* with you? What are you *doing*?" Bonnie was gasping in return. "Let go of me. Do you know what I had to do to get my mother to let me out of the house tonight? She wants to take me to the hospital at Roanoke."

Meredith kicked the door shut. "Okay," she said to Bonnie. "Now, you're going to see something that will . . . well, it's going to be a shock. But you can't scream, do you understand me? I'll let go of you if you promise."

"It's too dark to see anything, and you're scaring me. What's *wrong* with you, Meredith? Oh, all right, I promise, but what are you talking—"

"Elena," said Meredith. Elena took it as an invitation and stepped forward.

Bonnie's reaction wasn't what she expected. She frowned and leaned forward, peering in the dim light. When she saw Elena's form, she gasped. But then, as she stared at Elena's face, she clapped her hands together with a shriek of joy.

"I knew it! I knew they were wrong! So there, Meredith—and you and Stefan thought you knew so much about drowning and all that. But I knew you were wrong! Oh, Elena, I missed you! Everyone's going to be so—"

"Be *quiet*, Bonnie! Be quiet!" Meredith said urgently. "I told you not to scream. Listen, you idiot, do you think if Elena were really all right she'd be *here* in the middle of the night without anybody knowing about it?"

"But she *is* all right; look at her. She's standing there. It is you, isn't it, Elena?" Bonnie started toward her, but Meredith grabbed her again.

"Yes, it's me." Elena had the strange feeling she'd wandered into a surreal comedy, maybe one written by Kafka, only she didn't know her lines. She didn't know what to say to Bonnie, who was looking rapturous.

"It's me, but . . . I'm not exactly all right," she said awkwardly, sitting down again. Meredith nudged Bonnie to sit down on the bed.

"What are you two being so mysterious for? She's here, but she's not all right. What's that supposed to mean?"

Elena didn't know whether to laugh or cry. "Look, Bonnie . . . oh, I don't know how to say this. Bonnie, did your psychic grandmother ever talk to you about vampires?"

Silence fell, heavy as an ax. The minutes ticked by. Impossibly, Bonnie's eyes widened still further; then, they slid toward Meredith. There were several more minutes of silence, and then Bonnie shifted her weight toward the door. "Uh, look, you guys," she said softly, "this is getting really weird. I mean, really, really, really . . ."

Elena cast about in her mind. "You can look at my teeth," she said. She pulled her upper lip back, poking at a canine with her finger. She felt the reflexive lengthening and sharpening, like a cat's claw lazily extending.

Meredith came forward and looked and then looked away quickly. "I get the point," she said, but in her voice there was none of the old wry pleasure in her own wit. "Bonnie, look," she said.

All the elation, all the excitement had drained out of Bonnie. She looked as if she were going to be sick. "No. I don't want to."

"You have to. You have to believe it, or we'll never get anywhere." Meredith grappled a stiff and resisting Bonnie forward. "Open your eyes, you little twit. You're the one who loves all this supernatural stuff."

"I've changed my *mind*," Bonnie said, almost sobbing. There was genuine hysteria in her tone. "Leave me *alone*, Meredith; I don't *want* to look." She wrenched herself away.

"You don't have to," Elena whispered, stunned. Dismay pooled inside her, and tears flooded her eyes. "This was a bad idea, Meredith. I'll go away."

"*No.* Oh, don't." Bonnie turned back as quickly as she'd whirled away and precipi-

100

tated herself into Elena's arms. "I'm sorry, Elena; I'm sorry. I don't care what you are; I'm just glad you're back. It's been terrible without you." She was sobbing now in earnest.

The tears that wouldn't come when Elena had been with Stefan came now. She cried, holding on to Bonnie, feeling Meredith's arms go around both of them. They were all crying—Meredith silently, Bonnie noisily, and Elena herself with passionate intensity. She felt as if she were crying for everything that had happened to her, for everything she had lost, for all the loneliness and the fear and the pain.

Eventually, they all ended up sitting on the floor, knee to knee, the way they had when they were kids at a sleepover making secret plans.

"You're so brave," Bonnie said to Elena, sniffling. "I don't see how you can be so brave about it."

"You don't know how I'm feeling inside. I'm not brave at all. But I've got to deal with it somehow, because I don't know what else to do."

"Your hands aren't cold." Meredith

And she couldn't help her reaction, her frustrated, impotent rage. She started for him, and he caught her wrists and held her off, his eyes boring into hers. She was startled to hear the sound that came from her lips then; it was a hiss that sounded more feline than human. She realized her fingers were hooked into claws.

What am I doing? Attacking him because he won't defend people against the dogs that are attacking *them*? What kind of sense does that make? Breathing hard, she relaxed her hands and wet her lips. She stepped back and he let her.

There was a long moment while they stared at each other.

"I'm going down," Elena said quietly and turned.

"No."

"They need help."

"All right, then, damn you." She'd never heard Damon's voice so low, or so furious. "I'll—" he broke off and Elena, turning back quickly, saw him slam a fist into the window-sill, rattling the glass. But his attention was outside and his voice perfectly composed again when he said dryly, "Help has arrived."

It was the fire department. Their hoses

squeezed Elena's fingers. "Just sort of cool. I thought they'd be colder."

"Stefan's hands aren't cold either," Elena said, and she was about to go on, but Bonnie squeaked: "*Stefan?*"

Meredith and Elena looked at her.

"Be sensible, Bonnie. You don't get to be a vampire by yourself. Somebody has to make you one."

"But you mean *Stefan* . . . ? You mean he's a . . . ?" Bonnie's voice choked off.

"I think," said Meredith, "that maybe this is the time to tell us the whole story, Elena. Like all those minor details you left out the last time we asked you for the whole story."

Elena nodded. "You're right. It's hard to explain, but I'll try." She took a deep breath. "Bonnie, do you remember the first day of school? It was the first time I ever heard you make a prophecy. You looked into my palm and said I'd meet a boy, a dark boy, a stranger. And that he wasn't tall but that he *had* been once. Well"—she looked at Bonnie and then at Meredith—"Stefan's not really tall now. But he was once . . . compared to other people in the fifteenth century."

Meredith nodded, but Bonnie made a faint

sound and swayed backward, looking shell-shocked. "You mean—"

"I mean he lived in Renaissance Italy, and the average person was shorter then. So Stefan looked taller by comparison. And, wait, before you pass out, here's something else you should know. Damon's his brother."

Meredith nodded again. "I figured something like that. But then why has Damon been saying he's a college student?"

"They don't get along very well. For a long time, Stefan didn't even know Damon was in Fell's Church." Elena faltered. She was verging on Stefan's private history, which she'd always felt was *his* secret to tell. But Meredith had been right; it was time to come out with the whole story. "Listen, it was like this," she said. "Stefan and Damon were both in love with the same girl back in Renaissance Italy. She was from Germany, and her name was Katherine. The reason Stefan was avoiding me at the beginning of school was that I reminded him of her; she had blond hair and blue eyes, too. Oh, and this was her ring." Elena let go of Meredith's hand and showed them the intricately carved golden circlet set with a single stone of lapis lazuli.

"And the thing was that Katherine was a

vampire. A guy named Klaus had made her one back in her village in Germany to save her from dying of her last illness. Stefan and Damon both knew this, but they didn't care. They asked her to choose between them the one she wanted to marry." Elena stopped and gave a lopsided smile, thinking that Mr. Tanner had been right; history did repeat itself. She only hoped her story didn't end like Katherine's. "But she chose *both* of them. She exchanged blood with both of them, and she said they could all three be companions through eternity."

"Sounds kinky," murmured Bonnie.

"Sounds *dumb*," said Meredith.

"You got it," Elena told her. "Katherine was sweet but not very bright. Stefan and Damon already didn't like each other. They told her she *had* to choose, that they wouldn't even think of sharing her. And she ran off crying. The next day—well, they found her body, or what was left of it. See, a vampire needs a talisman like this ring to go out in the sun without being killed. And Katherine went out in the sun and took hers off. She thought if she were out of the way, Damon and Stefan would be reconciled."

"Oh, my God, how ro—"

"No, it *isn't*," Elena cut Bonnie off savagely. "It's not romantic at all. Stefan's been living with the guilt ever since, and I think Damon has, too, although you'd never get him to admit it. And the immediate result was that they got a couple of swords and killed each other. Yes, *killed*. That's why they're vampires now, and that's why they hate each other so much. And that's why I'm probably crazy trying to get them to cooperate now."

Seven

"To cooperate at what?" Meredith asked.

"I'll explain about that later. But first I want to know what's been going on in town since I—left."

"Well, hysteria mostly," Meredith said, raising an eyebrow. "Your Aunt Judith's been pretty badly off. She hallucinated that she saw you—only it wasn't a hallucination, was it? And she and Robert have sort of broken up."

"I know," Elena said grimly. "Go on."

"Everybody at school is upset. I wanted to talk to Stefan, especially when I began to suspect you weren't really dead, but he hasn't been at school. Matt *has* been, but there's something wrong with him. He looks like a zombie, and he won't talk to anyone. I wanted to explain to him that there was a chance you might not be gone forever; I thought that would cheer him up. But he wouldn't listen. He was acting totally out of character, and at one point I thought he was going to hit me. He wouldn't listen to a word."

"Oh, God—Matt." Something terrible was stirring at the bottom of Elena's mind, some memory too disturbing to be let loose. She couldn't cope with anything more just now, she *couldn't*, she thought, and slam dunked the memory back down.

Meredith was going on. "It's clear, though, that some other people are suspicious about your 'death.' That's why I said what I did in the memorial service; I was afraid if I said the real day and place that Alaric Saltzman would end up ambushing you outside the house. He's been asking all sorts of questions, and it's a good thing Bonnie didn't know anything she could blab."

"That isn't fair," Bonnie protested. "Alaric's just interested, that's all, and he wants to help us through the trauma, like before. He's an Aquarius—"

"He's a spy," said Elena, "and maybe more than that. But we'll talk about that later.

What about Tyler Smallwood? I didn't see him at the service."

Meredith looked nonplussed. "You mean you don't know?"

"I don't know *anything*; I've been asleep for four days in an attic."

"Well . . ." Meredith paused uneasily. "Tyler just got back from the hospital. Same with Dick Carter and those four tough guys they had along with them on Founders' Day. They were attacked in the Quonset hut that evening and they lost a lot of blood."

"*Oh.*" The mystery of why Stefan's Powers had been so much stronger that night was explained. And why they'd been getting weaker ever since. He probably hadn't eaten since then. "Meredith, is Stefan a suspect?"

"Well, Tyler's father tried to make him one, but the police couldn't make the times work out. They know approximately when Tyler was attacked because he was supposed to meet Mr. Smallwood, and he didn't show up. And Bonnie and I can alibi Stefan for that time because we'd just left him by the river with your body. So he *couldn't* have gotten back to the Quonset hut to attack Tyler—at least no normal human could. And so far the police aren't thinking about anything supernatural."

"I see." Elena felt relieved on that score at least.

"Tyler and those guys can't identify the attacker because they can't remember a thing about that afternoon," Meredith added. "Neither can Caroline."

"*Caroline* was in there?"

"Yes, but she wasn't bitten. Just in shock. In spite of everything she's done, I almost feel sorry for her." Meredith shrugged and added, "She looks pretty pathetic these days."

"And I don't think anyone will ever suspect Stefan after what happened with those dogs at church today," Bonnie put in. "My dad says that a big dog could have broken the window in the Quonset hut, and the wounds in Tyler's throat looked sort of like animal wounds. I think a lot of people believe it was a dog or a pack of dogs that did it."

"It's a convenient explanation," Meredith said dryly. "It means they don't have to think any more about it."

"But that's ridiculous," said Elena. "Normal dogs don't behave that way. Aren't people wondering about *why* their dogs would suddenly go mad and turn on them?"

"Lots of people are just getting rid of them. Oh, and I heard someone talk about mandatory rabies testing," Meredith said. "But it's not just rabies, is it, Elena?"

"No, I don't think so. And neither do Stefan or Damon. And that's what I came over to talk to you about." Elena explained, as clearly as she could, what she had been thinking about the Other Power in Fell's Church. She told about the force that had chased her off the bridge and about the feeling she'd had with the dogs and about everything she and Stefan and Damon had discussed. She finished with, "And Bonnie said it herself in church today: 'Something evil.' I think that's what's here in Fell's Church, something nobody knows about, something completely evil. I don't suppose *you* know what you meant by that, Bonnie."

But Bonnie's mind was running on another track. "So Damon didn't *necessarily* do all those awful things you said he did," she said shrewdly. "Like killing Yangtze and hurting Vickie and murdering Mr. Tanner, and all. I told you nobody that gorgeous could be a psycho killer."

"I think," said Meredith with a glance at

Elena, "that you had better forget about Damon as a love interest."

"Yes," said Elena emphatically. "He *did* kill Mr. Tanner, Bonnie. And it stands to reason he did the other attacks, too; I'll ask him about that. And I'm having enough trouble dealing with him myself. You don't want to mess with him, Bonnie, believe me."

"I'm supposed to leave Damon alone; I'm supposed to leave Alaric alone. . . . Are there any guys I'm *not* supposed to leave alone? And meanwhile Elena gets them all. It's not fair."

"*Life* isn't fair," Meredith told her callously. "But listen, Elena, even if this Other Power exists, what sort of power do you think it is? What does it look like?"

"I don't know. Something tremendously strong—but it could be shielding itself so that we can't sense it. It could look like an ordinary person. And that's why I came for your help, because it could be anybody in Fell's Church. It's like what Bonnie said during the service today: 'Nobody is what they seem.'"

Bonnie looked forlorn. "I don't remember saying that."

"You said it, all right. 'Nobody is what they seem,'" Elena quoted again weightily. "*No-*

body.'' She glanced at Meredith, but the dark eyes under the elegantly arched eyebrows were calm and distant.

"Well, that would seem to make *everybody* a suspect," Meredith said in her most unruffled voice. "Right?"

"Right," said Elena. "But we'd better get a note pad and pencil and make a list of the most important ones. Damon and Stefan have already agreed to help investigate, and if you'll help, too, we'll stand an even better chance of finding it." She was hitting her stride with this; she'd always been good at organizing things, from schemes to get boys to fundraising events. This was just a more serious version of the old plan A and plan B.

Meredith gave the pencil and paper to Bonnie, who looked at it, and then at Meredith, and then at Elena. "Fine," she said, "but who goes *on* the list?"

"Well, anyone we have reason to suspect of being the Other Power. Anyone who might have done the things we know it did: seal Stefan in the well, chase me, set those dogs on people. Anyone we've noticed behaving oddly."

"Matt," said Bonnie, writing busily. "And Vickie. And Robert."

"Bonnie!" exclaimed Elena and Meredith simultaneously.

Bonnie looked up. "Well, Matt *has* been acting oddly, and so has Vickie, for months now. And Robert was hanging around outside the church before the service, but he never came in—"

"Oh, Bonnie, honestly," Meredith said. "Vickie's a *victim*, not a suspect. And if Matt's an evil Power, I'm the hunchback of Notre Dame. And as for Robert—"

"Fine, I've crossed it all out," said Bonnie coldly. "Now let's hear *your* ideas."

"No, wait," Elena said. "Bonnie, wait a moment." She was thinking about something, something that had been nagging at her for quite a while, ever since— "Ever since the church," she said aloud, remembering it. "Do you know, I saw Robert outside the church, too, when I was hidden in the choir loft. It was just before the dogs attacked, and he was sort of backing away like he knew what was going to happen."

"Oh, but Elena—"

"No, listen, Meredith. And I saw him before, on Saturday night, with Aunt Judith. When she told him she wouldn't marry him there was something in his face. . . . I don't know. But I think you'd better put him back on the list, Bonnie."

Soberly, after a moment's hesitation, Bonnie did. "Who else?" she said.

"Well, Alaric, I'm afraid," Elena said. "I'm sorry, Bonnie, but he's practically number one." She told what she had overheard that morning between Alaric and the principal. "He isn't a normal history teacher; they called him here for some reason. He knows I'm a vampire, and he's looking for me. And today, while the dogs were attacking, he was standing there on the sidelines making some kind of weird gestures. He's definitely not what he seems, and the only question is: what *is* he? Are you listening, Meredith?"

"Yes. You know, I think you should put Mrs. Flowers on that list. Remember the way she stood at the window of the boardinghouse when we were bringing Stefan back from the well? But she wouldn't come downstairs to open the door for us? That's odd behavior."

Elena nodded. "Yes, and how she kept hanging up on me when I called him. And she certainly keeps to herself in that old house. She may just be a dotty old lady, but put her down anyway, Bonnie." She ran a hand through her hair, lifting it off the back of her neck. She was hot. Or—not hot exactly, but uncomfortable in some way that was similar to being overheated. She felt parched.

"All right, we'll go by the boardinghouse tomorrow before school," Meredith said. "Meanwhile, what else can we be doing? Let's have a look at that list, Bonnie."

Bonnie held the list out so they could see it, and Elena and Meredith leaned forward and read:

~~Matt Honeycutt~~
~~Vickie Bennett~~
Robert Maxwell—What was he doing at the church when the dogs attacked? And what was going on that night with Elena's aunt?
Alaric Saltzman—Why does he ask so many questions? What was he called to Fell's Church to do?
Mrs. Flowers—Why does she act so strange? Why didn't she let us in the night Stefan was wounded?

"Good," Elena said. "I guess we could also find out whose dogs were at the church today. And you can watch Alaric at school tomorrow."

"*I'll* watch Alaric," Bonnie said firmly. "And I'll get him cleared of suspicion; you see if I don't."

"Fine, you do that. You can be assigned to him. And Meredith can investigate Mrs. Flowers, and I can take Robert. And as for Stefan and Damon—well, they can be assigned to *everyone*, because they can use their Powers to probe people's minds. Besides, that list is by no means complete. I'm going to ask them to scout around town searching for any signs of Power, or anything else weird going on. They're more likely than I am to recognize it."

Sitting back, Elena wet her lips absently. She *was* parched. She noticed something she'd never noticed before: the fine tracery of veins on Bonnie's inner wrist. Bonnie was still holding the note pad out, and the skin of her wrist was so translucent that the teal blue veins showed clearly through. Elena wished she'd listened when they'd studied human anatomy at school; now what was the name for this vein, the big one that branched like a fork in a tree . . . ?

"Elena. Elena!"

Startled, Elena looked up, to see Meredith's wary dark eyes and Bonnie's alarmed expression. It was only then that she realized she was crouched close to Bonnie's wrist, rubbing the biggest vein with her finger.

"Sorry," she murmured, sitting back. But she could feel the extra length and sharpness of her canine teeth. It was something like wearing braces; she could clearly feel the difference in weight. She realized her reassuring smile at Bonnie was not having the desired effect. Bonnie was looking scared, which was silly. Bonnie ought to know that Elena would never hurt her. And Elena wasn't *very* hungry tonight; Elena had always been a light eater. She could get all she needed from this tiny vein here in the wrist. . . .

Elena jumped to her feet and spun toward the window, leaning against the casing, feeling the cool night air blowing on her skin. She felt dizzy, and she couldn't seem to get her breath.

What had she been *doing?* She turned around to see Bonnie huddled close to Meredith, both of them looking sick with fear. She hated having them look at her that way.

"I'm sorry," she said. "I didn't mean to, Bonnie. Look, I'm not coming any closer. I should have eaten before I came here. Damon said I'd get hungry later."

Bonnie swallowed, looking even sicker. "Eaten?"

"Yes, of course," Elena said tartly. Her veins were burning; that was what this feeling was. Stefan had described it before, but she'd never really understood; she'd never realized what he was going through when the need for blood was on him. It was terrible, irresistible. "What do you think I eat these days, air?" she added defiantly. "I'm a hunter now, and I'd better go out hunting."

Bonnie and Meredith were trying to cope; she could tell they were, but she could also see the revulsion in their eyes. She concentrated on using her new senses, in opening herself to the night and searching for Stefan's or Damon's presence. It was difficult, because neither of them was projecting with his mind as he had been the night they'd been fighting in the woods, but she thought she could sense a glimmer of Power out there in the town.

But she had no way to communicate with it, and frustration made the scorching in her veins even worse. She'd just decided that she might have to go without them when the curtains whipped back into her face, flapping in a burst of wind. Bonnie lurched up with a gasp, knocking the reading lamp off the nightstand and plunging the room into darkness. Cursing, Meredith worked to get it righted again. The curtains fluttered madly in the flickering light that emerged, and Bonnie seemed to be trying to scream.

When the bulb was finally screwed back in, it revealed Damon sitting casually but precariously on the sill of the open window, one knee up. He was smiling one of his wildest smiles.

"Do you mind?" he said. "This is uncomfortable."

Elena glanced back at Bonnie and Meredith, who were braced against the closet, looking horrified and hypnotized at once. She herself shook her head, exasperated.

"And I thought *I* liked to make a dramatic entrance," she said. "Very funny, Damon. Now let's go."

"With two such beautiful friends of yours right here?" Damon smiled again at Bonnie and Meredith. "Besides, I only just got here. Won't somebody be polite and ask me in?"

Bonnie's brown eyes, fixed helplessly on his face, softened a bit. Her lips, which had been parted in horror, parted further. Elena recognized the signs of imminent meltdown.

"No, they *won't*," she said. She put herself

directly between Damon and the other girls. "Nobody here is for you, Damon—not now, not ever." Seeing the flare of challenge in his eyes, she added archly, "And anyway, I'm leaving. I don't know about *you*, but I'm going hunting." She was reassured to sense Stefan's presence nearby, on the roof probably, and to hear his instant amendment: *We're going hunting, Damon. You can sit there all night if you want.*

Damon gave in with good grace, shooting one last amused glance toward Bonnie before disappearing from the window. Bonnie and Meredith both started forward in alarm as he did, obviously concerned that he had just fallen to his death.

"He's fine," said Elena, shaking her head again. "And don't worry, I won't let him come back. I'll meet you at the same time tomorrow. Good-bye."

"But—Elena—" Meredith stopped. "I mean, I was going to ask you if you wanted to change your clothes."

Elena regarded herself. The nineteenth-century heirloom dress was tattered and bedraggled, the thin white muslin shredded in some places. But there was no time to change it; she had to feed *now*.

"It'll have to wait," she said. "See you tomorrow." And she boosted herself out of the window the way Damon had. The last she saw of them, Meredith and Bonnie were staring after her dazedly.

She was getting better at landings; this time she didn't bruise her knees. Stefan was there, and he wrapped something dark and warm around her.

"Your cloak," she said, pleased. For a moment they smiled at each other, remembering the first time he had given her the cloak, after he'd saved her from Tyler in the graveyard and taken her back to his room to clean up. He'd been afraid to touch her then. But, Elena thought, smiling up into his eyes, she had taken care of that fear rather quickly.

"I thought we were hunting," Damon said.

Elena turned the smile on him, without unlinking her hand from Stefan's. "We are," she said. "Where should we go?"

"Any house on this street," Damon suggested.

"The woods," Stefan said.

"The woods," Elena decided. "We don't touch humans, and we don't kill. Isn't that how it goes, Stefan?"

He returned the pressure of her fingers. "That's how it goes," he said quietly.

Damon's lip curled fastidiously. "And just what are we looking for in the woods, or don't I want to know? Muskrat? Skunk? Termites?" His eyes moved to Elena and his voice dropped. "Come with me, and I'll show you some real hunting."

"We can go through the graveyard," Elena said, ignoring him.

"White-tailed deer feed all night in the open areas," Stefan told her, "but we'll have to be careful stalking them; they can hear almost as well as we can."

Another time, then, Damon's voice said in Elena's mind.

Eight

"Who——? Oh, it's you!" Bonnie said, starting at the touch on her elbow. "You scared me. I didn't hear you come up."

He'd have to be more careful, Stefan realized. In the few days he'd been away from school, he'd gotten out of the habit of walking and moving like a human and fallen back into the noiseless, perfectly controlled stride of the hunter. "Sorry," he said, as they walked side by side down the corridor.

"S'okay," said Bonnie with a brave attempt at nonchalance. But her brown eyes were wide and rather fixed. "So what are you doing here today? Meredith and I came by the boardinghouse this morning to check on Mrs.

Flowers, but nobody answered the door. And I didn't see you in biology."

"I came this afternoon. I'm back at school. For as long as it takes to find what we're looking for anyway."

"To spy on Alaric, you mean," Bonnie muttered. "I told Elena yesterday just to leave him to me. Oops," she added, as a couple of passing juniors stared at her. She rolled her eyes at Stefan. By mutual consent, they turned off into a side corridor and made for an empty stairwell. Bonnie leaned against the wall with a groan of relief.

"I've got to remember not to say her name," she said pathetically, "but it's so *hard.* My mother asked me how I felt this morning and I almost told her, 'fine,' since I saw Elena last night. I don't know how you two kept—you know what—a secret so long."

Stefan felt a grin tugging at his lips in spite of himself. Bonnie was like a six-week-old kitten, all charm and no inhibitions. She always said exactly what she was thinking at the moment, even if it completely contradicted what she'd just said the moment before, but everything she did came from the heart. "You're standing in a deserted hallway with a you

know what right now," he reminded her dev-
ilishly.

"Ohhh." Her eyes widened again. "But you
wouldn't, would you?" she added, relieved.
"Because Elena would *kill* you. . . . Oh,
dear." Searching for another topic, she
gulped and said, "So—so how did things go
last night?"

Stefan's mood darkened immediately. "Not
so good. Oh, Elena's all right; she's sleeping
safely." Before he could go on, his ears picked
up footfalls at the end of the corridor. Three
senior girls were passing by, and one broke
away from the group at the sight of Stefan
and Bonnie. Sue Carson's face was pale and
her eyes were red-rimmed, but she smiled at
them.

Bonnie was full of concern. "Sue, how are
you? How's Doug?"

"I'm okay. He's okay, too, or at least he's
going to be. Stefan, I wanted to talk to you,"
she added in a rush. "I know my dad thanked
you yesterday for helping Doug the way you
did, but I wanted to thank you, too. I mean, I
know that people in town have been pretty
horrible to you and—well, I'm just surprised
you cared enough to help at all. But I'm glad.
My mom says you saved Doug's life. And so, I

just wanted to thank you, and to say I'm sorry —about everything."

Her voice was shaking by the end of the speech. Bonnie sniffed and groped in her backpack for a tissue, and for a moment it looked as if Stefan was going to be caught on the stairwell with two sobbing females. Dismayed, he racked his brains for a distraction.

"That's all right," he said. "How's Chelsea today?"

"She's at the pound. They're holding the dogs in quarantine there, all the ones they could round up." Sue blotted her eyes and straightened, and Stefan relaxed, seeing that the danger was over. An awkward silence descended.

"Well," said Bonnie to Sue at last, "have you heard what the school board decided about the Snow Dance?"

"I heard they met this morning and they've pretty much decided to let us have it. Somebody said they were talking about a police guard, though. Oh, there's the late bell. We'd better get to history before Alaric hands us all demerits."

"We're coming in a minute," Stefan said. He added casually, "When is this Snow Dance?"

"It's the thirteenth; Friday night, you know," Sue said, and then winced. "Oh my God, Friday the thirteenth. I didn't even think about that. But it reminds me that there was one other thing I wanted to tell you. This morning I took my name out of the running for snow queen. It—it just seemed right, somehow. That's all." Sue hurried away, almost running.

Stefan's mind was racing. "Bonnie, *what* is this Snow Dance?"

"Well, it's the Christmas dance really, only we have a snow queen instead of a Christmas queen. After what happened at Founders' Day, they were thinking of canceling it, and then with the dogs yesterday—but it sounds like they're going to have it after all."

"On Friday the thirteenth," Stefan said grimly.

"Yes." Bonnie was looking scared again, making herself small and inconspicuous. "Stefan, don't look that way; you're frightening me. What's wrong? What do you think will happen at the dance?"

"I don't know." But something would, Stefan was thinking. Fell's Church hadn't had one public celebration that had escaped being visited by the Other Power, and this would probably be the last festivity of the year. But there was no point in talking about it now. "Come on," he said. "We're really late."

He was right. Alaric Saltzman was at the chalkboard when they walked in, as he had been the first day he'd appeared in the history classroom. If he was surprised at seeing them late, or at all, he covered it faultlessly, giving one of his friendliest smiles.

So you're the one who's hunting the hunter, Stefan thought, taking his seat and studying the man before him. But are you anything more than that? Elena's Other Power maybe?

On the face of it, nothing seemed more unlikely. Alaric's sandy hair, worn just a little too long for a teacher, his boyish smile, his stubborn cheerfulness, all contributed to an impression of harmlessness. But Stefan had been wary from the beginning of what was under that inoffensive exterior. Still, it didn't seem very likely that Alaric Saltzman was behind the attack on Elena or the incident with the dogs. No disguise could be that perfect.

Elena. Stefan's hand clenched under his desk, and a slow ache woke in his chest. He hadn't meant to think about her. The only way he had gotten through the last five days was by keeping her at the edge of his mind, not letting her image any closer. But then of course the effort of holding her away at a safe distance took up most of his time and energy. And this was the worst place of all to be, in a classroom where he couldn't care less about what was being taught. There was nothing to do *but* think here.

He made himself breathe slowly, calmly. She was well; that was the important thing. Nothing else really mattered. But even as he told himself this, jealousy bit into him like the thongs of a whip. Because whenever he thought about Elena now, he had to think about *him.*

About Damon, who was free to come and go as he liked. Who might even be with Elena this minute.

Anger burned in Stefan's mind, bright and cold, mingling with the hot ache in his chest. He still wasn't convinced that Damon wasn't the one who had casually thrown him, bleeding and unconscious, into an abandoned well shaft to die. And he would take Elena's idea about the Other Power much more seriously if he was completely sure that Damon hadn't chased Elena to her death. Damon was evil; he had no mercy and no scruples. . . .

And what's he done that I haven't done? Stefan asked himself heavily, for the hundredth time. Nothing.

Except kill.

Stefan had tried to kill. He'd meant to kill Tyler. At the memory, the cold fire of his anger toward Damon was doused, and he glanced instead toward a desk at the back of the room.

It was empty. Though Tyler had gotten out of the hospital the day before, he hadn't returned to school. Still, there should be no danger of his remembering anything from that grisly afternoon. The subliminal suggestion to forget should hold for quite a while, as long as no one messed with Tyler's mind.

He suddenly became aware that he was staring at Tyler's empty desk with narrow, brooding eyes. As he looked away, he caught the glance of someone who'd been watching him do it.

Matt turned quickly and bent over his history book, but not before Stefan saw his expression.

Don't think about it. Don't think about anything, Stefan told himself, and he tried to concentrate on Alaric Saltzman's lecture about the Wars of the Roses.

December 5—I don't know what time, probably early afternoon.
Dear Diary,

Damon got you back for me this morning. Stefan said he didn't want me going into Alaric's attic again. This is Stefan's pen I'm using. I don't own anything anymore, or at least I can't get at any of my own things, and most of them Aunt Judith would miss if I took them. I'm sitting right now in a barn behind the boardinghouse. I can't go where people sleep, you know, unless I've been invited in. I guess animals don't count, because there are some rats sleeping here under the hay and an owl in the rafters. At the moment, we're ignoring each other.

I'm trying very hard not to have hysterics.

I thought writing might help. Something normal, something familiar. Except that nothing in my life is normal anymore.

Damon says I'll get used to it faster if I throw my old life away and embrace the new one. He seems to think it's inevitable that I turn out like him. He says I was born to be a hunter and there's no point in doing things halfway.

I hunted a deer last night. A stag, because it

was making the most noise, clashing its antlers against tree branches, challenging other males. I drank its blood.

When I look over this diary, all I can see is that I was searching for something, for someplace to belong. But this isn't it. This new life isn't it. I'm afraid of what I'll become if I do start to belong here.

Oh, God, I'm frightened.

The barn owl is almost pure white, especially when it spreads its wings so you can see the underside. From the back it looks more gold. It has just a little gold around the face. It's staring at me right now because I'm making noises, trying not to cry.

It's funny that I can still cry. I guess it's witches that can't.

It's started snowing outside. I'm pulling my cloak up around me.

Elena tucked the little book close to her body and drew the soft dark velvet of the cloak up to her chin. The barn was utterly silent, except for the minute breathing of the animals that slept there. Outside the snow drifted down just as soundlessly, blanketing the world in muffling stillness. Elena stared at it with unseeing eyes, scarcely noticing the tears that ran down her cheeks.

* * *

"And could Bonnie McCullough and Caroline Forbes please stay after class a moment," Alaric said as the last bell rang.

Stefan frowned, a frown that deepened as he saw Vickie Bennett hovering outside the open door of the history room, her eyes shy and frightened. "I'll be right outside," he said meaningfully to Bonnie, who nodded. He added a warning lift of his eyebrows, and she responded with a virtuous look. Catch *me* saying anything I'm not supposed to, the look said.

Going out, Stefan only hoped she could stick to it.

Vickie Bennett was entering as he exited, and he had to step out of her way. But that took him right into the path of Matt, who'd come out the other door and was trying to get down the corridor as fast as possible.

Stefan grabbed his arm without thinking. "Matt, wait."

"Let go of me." Matt's fist came up. He looked at it in apparent surprise, as if not sure what he should be so mad about. But every muscle in his body was fighting Stefan's grip.

"I just want to talk to you. Just for a minute, all right?"

"I don't have a minute," Matt said, and at last his eyes, a lighter, less complicated blue than Elena's, met Stefan's. But there was a blankness in the depths of them that reminded Stefan of the look of someone who'd been hypnotized, or who was under the influence of some Power.

Only it was no Power except Matt's own mind, he realized abruptly. This was what the human brain did to itself when faced with something it simply couldn't deal with. Matt had shut down, turned off.

Testing, Stefan said, "About what happened Saturday night—"

"I don't know what you're talking about. Look, I said I had to go, damn it." Denial was like a fortress behind Matt's eyes. But Stefan had to try again.

"I don't blame you for being mad. If I were you, I'd be furious. And I know what it's like not to want to think, especially when thinking can drive you crazy." Matt was shaking his head, and Stefan looked around the hallway. It was almost empty, and desperation made him willing to take a risk. He lowered his voice. "But maybe you'd at least like to know that Elena's awake, and she's much—"

"Elena's dead!" Matt shouted, drawing the

attention of everyone in the corridor. "And I told you to let go of me!" he added, oblivious of their audience, and shoved Stefan hard. It was so unexpected that Stefan stumbled back against the lockers, almost ending up sprawled on the ground. He stared at Matt, but Matt never even glanced back as he took off down the hallway.

Stefan spent the rest of the time until Bonnie emerged just staring at the wall. There was a poster there for the Snow Dance, and he knew every inch of it by the time the girls came out.

Despite everything Caroline had tried to do to him and Elena, Stefan found he couldn't summon up any hatred of her. Her auburn hair looked faded, her face pinched. Instead of being willowy, her posture just looked wilted, he thought, watching her go.

"Everything okay?" he said to Bonnie, as they fell into step with each other.

"Yes, of course. Alaric just knows we three —Vickie, Caroline, and I—have been through a lot, and he wants *us* to know that he supports us," Bonnie said, but even her dogged optimism about the history teacher sounded a little forced. "None of us told him about anything, though. He's having another get-together at his house next week," she added brightly.

Wonderful, thought Stefan. Normally he might have said something about it, but at that moment he was distracted. "There's Meredith," he said.

"She must be waiting for us—no, she's going down the history wing," Bonnie said. "That's funny, I told her I'd meet her out here."

It was more than funny, thought Stefan. He'd caught only a glimpse of her as she turned the corner, but that glimpse stuck in his mind. The expression on Meredith's face had been calculating, watchful, and her step had been stealthy. As if she were trying to do something without being seen.

"She'll come back in a minute when she sees we're not down there," Bonnie said, but Meredith didn't come back in a minute, or two, or three. In fact, it was almost ten minutes before she appeared, and then she looked startled to see Stefan and Bonnie waiting for her.

"Sorry, I got held up," she said coolly, and Stefan had to admire her self-possession. But he wondered what was behind it, and only

Bonnie was in a mood to chat as the three of them left school.

"But last time you used fire," Elena said.

"That was because we were looking for Stefan, for a specific person," Bonnie replied. "This time we're trying to predict the future. If it was just *your* personal future I was trying to predict, I'd look in your palm, but we're trying to find out something general."

Meredith entered the room, carefully balancing a china bowl full to the brim with water. In her other hand, she held a candle. "I've got the stuff," she said.

"Water was sacred to the Druids," Bonnie explained, as Meredith placed the dish on the floor and the three girls sat around it.

"Apparently, *everything* was sacred to the Druids," said Meredith.

"Shh. Now, put the candle in the candlestick and light it. Then I'm going to pour melted wax into the water, and the shapes it makes will tell me the answers to your questions. My grandmother used melted lead, and she said *her* grandmother used melted silver, but she told me wax would do." When Meredith had lit the candle, Bonnie glanced at it sideways and took a deep breath. "I'm getting scareder and scareder to do this," she said.

"You don't have to," Elena said softly.

"I know. But I want to—this once. Besides, it's not these kind of rituals that scare me; it's getting taken over that's so awful. I *hate* it. It's like somebody else getting into my body."

Elena frowned and opened her mouth, but Bonnie was continuing.

"Anyway, here goes. Turn down the lights, Meredith. Give me a minute to get attuned and then ask your questions."

In the silence of the dim room Elena watched the candlelight flickering over Bonnie's lowered eyelashes and Meredith's sober face. She looked down at her own hands in her lap, pale against the blackness of the sweater and leggings Meredith had lent her. Then she looked at the dancing flame.

"All right," Bonnie said softly and took the candle.

Elena's fingers twined together, clenching hard, but she spoke in a low voice so as not to break the atmosphere. "Who is the Other Power in Fell's Church?"

Bonnie tilted the candle so that the flame licked up its sides. Hot wax streamed down like water into the bowl and formed round globules there.

"I was afraid of that," Bonnie murmured. "That's no answer, nothing. Try a different question."

Disappointed, Elena sat back, fingernails biting into her palms. It was Meredith who spoke.

"Can *we* find this Other Power if we look? And can we defeat it?"

"That's two questions," Bonnie said under her breath as she tilted the candle again. This time the wax formed a circle, a lumpy white ring.

"That's unity! The symbol for people joining hands. It means we can do it if we stick together."

Elena's head jerked up. Those were almost the same words she'd said to Stefan and Damon. Bonnie's eyes were shining with excitement, and they smiled at each other.

"Watch out! You're still pouring," Meredith said.

Bonnie quickly righted the candle, looking into the bowl again. The last spill of wax had formed a thin, straight line.

"That's a sword," she said slowly. "It

means sacrifice. We can do it if we stick together, but not without sacrifice."

"What kind of sacrifice?" asked Elena.

"I don't know," Bonnie said, her face troubled. "That's all I can tell you this time." She stuck the candle back in the candleholder.

"Whew," said Meredith, as she got up to turn on the lights. Elena stood, too.

"Well, at least we know we can beat it," she said, tugging up the leggings, which were too long for her. She caught a glimpse of herself in Meredith's mirror. She certainly didn't look like Elena Gilbert the high school fashion plate anymore. Dressed all in black like this, she looked pale and dangerous, like a sheathed sword. Her hair fell haphazardly around her shoulders.

"They wouldn't know me at school," she murmured, with a pang. It was strange that she should care about going to school, but she did. It was because she *couldn't* go, she guessed. And because she'd been queen there so long, she'd run things for so long, that it was almost unbelievable that she could never set foot there again.

"You could go somewhere else," Bonnie suggested. "I mean, after this is all over, you could finish the school year someplace where nobody knows you. Like Stefan did."

"No, I don't think so." Elena was in a strange mood tonight, after spending the day alone in the barn watching the snow. "Bonnie," she said abruptly, "would you look at my palm again? I want you to tell *my* future, my personal future."

"I don't even know if I remember all the stuff my grandmother taught me . . . but, all right, I'll try," Bonnie relented. "There'd just better be no *more* dark strangers on the way, that's all. You've already got all you can handle." She giggled as she took Elena's outstretched hand. "Remember when Caroline asked what you could do with two? I guess you're finding out now, huh?"

"Just read my palm, will you?"

"All right, this is your life line—" Bonnie's stream of patter broke off almost before it was started. She stared at Elena's hand, fear and apprehension in her face. "It should go all the way down to here," she said. "But it's cut off so short. . . ."

She and Elena looked at each other without speaking for a moment, while Elena felt that same apprehension solidify inside herself. Then Meredith broke in.

"Well, naturally it's short," she said. "It just means what happened already, when Elena drowned."

"Yes, of course, that must be it," Bonnie murmured. She let go of Elena's hand and Elena slowly drew back. "That's it, all right," Bonnie said in a stronger voice.

Elena was gazing into the mirror again. The girl who gazed back was beautiful, but there was a sad wisdom about her eyes that the old Elena Gilbert had never had. She realized that Bonnie and Meredith were looking at her.

"That must be it," she said lightly, but her smile didn't touch her eyes.

Nine

"Well, at least I didn't get taken over," Bonnie said. "But I'm sick of this psychic stuff anyway; I'm tired of the whole thing. That was the last time, absolutely the last."

"All right," said Elena, turning away from the mirror, "let's talk about something else. Did you find anything out today?"

"I talked with Alaric, and he's having another get-together next week," Bonnie replied. "He asked Caroline and Vickie and me if we wanted to be hypnotized to help us deal with what's been happening. But I'm sure he isn't the Other Power, Elena. He's too nice."

Elena nodded. She'd had second thoughts about her suspicions of Alaric herself. Not because he was nice, but because she had spent four days in his attic asleep. Would the Other Power really have let her stay there unharmed? Of course, Damon had said he'd influenced Alaric to forget that she was up there, but would the Other Power have succumbed to Damon's influence? Shouldn't it be far too strong?

Unless its Powers had temporarily burned out, she thought suddenly. The way Stefan's were burning out now. Or unless it had only been *pretending* to be influenced.

"Well, we won't cross him off the list just yet," she said. "We've got to be careful. What about Mrs. Flowers? Did you find out anything about her?"

"No luck," said Meredith. "We went to the boardinghouse this morning, but she didn't answer the door. Stefan said he'd try to track her down in the afternoon."

"If somebody would only invite me *in* there, I could watch her, too," Elena said. "I feel like I'm the only one not doing anything. I think . . ." She paused a moment, considering, and then said, "I think I'll go by home —by Aunt Judith's, I mean. Maybe I'll find Robert hanging around in the bushes or something."

"We'll go with you," Meredith said.

"No, it's better for me to do it alone. Really, it is. I can be very inconspicuous these days."

"Then take your own advice and be careful. It's still snowing hard."

Elena nodded and dropped over the windowsill.

As she approached her house, she saw that a car was just pulling out of the driveway. She melted into the shadows and watched. The headlights illuminated an eerie winter sight: the neighbors' black locust tree, like a bare-branched silhouette, with a white owl sitting in it.

As the car roared past, Elena recognized it. Robert's blue Oldsmobile.

Now, *that* was interesting. She had an urge to follow him, but a stronger urge to check the house, make sure everything was all right. She circled it stealthily, examining windows.

The yellow chintz curtains at the kitchen window were looped back, revealing a bright section of kitchen inside. Aunt Judith was closing the dishwasher. Had Robert come to dinner? Elena wondered.

Aunt Judith moved toward the front hallway and Elena moved with her, circling the house again. She found a slit in the living room curtains and cautiously applied her eye to the thick, wavery old glass of the window. She heard the front door open and shut, and then lock, and then Aunt Judith came into the living room and sat on the couch. She switched on the TV and began flipping through channels idly.

Elena wished she could see more than just her aunt's profile in the flickering light of the TV. It gave her a strange feeling to look at this room, knowing that she could *only* look and not go in. How long had it been since she realized what a nice room it was? The old mahogany whatnot, crowded with china and glassware, the Tiffany lamp on the table next to Aunt Judith, the needlepoint pillows on the couch, all seemed precious to her now. Standing outside, feeling the feathery caress of the snow on the back of her neck, she wished she could go in just for a moment, just for a little while.

Aunt Judith's head was tilting back, her eyes shutting. Elena leaned her forehead against the window, then slowly turned away.

She climbed the quince tree outside her own bedroom, but to her disappointment the curtains were shut tight. The maple tree outside Margaret's room was fragile and harder to climb, but once she got up she had a good view; these curtains were wide open. Margaret was asleep with the bedcovers drawn up to her chin, her mouth open, her pale hair spread out like a fan on the pillow.

Hello, baby, Elena thought and swallowed back tears. It was such a sweetly innocent scene: the nightlight, the little girl in bed, the stuffed animals on the shelves keeping watch over her. And here came a little white kitten padding through the open door to complete the picture, Elena thought.

Snowball jumped onto Margaret's bed. The kitten yawned, showing a tiny pink tongue, and stretched, displaying miniature claws. Then it walked daintily over to stand on Margaret's chest.

Something tingled at the roots of Elena's hair.

She didn't know if it was some new hunter's sense or sheer intuition, but suddenly she was afraid. There was danger in that room. Margaret was in danger.

The kitten was still standing there, tail swishing back and forth. And all at once Elena realized what it looked like. The dogs. It looked the way Chelsea had looked at Doug Carson before she lunged at him. Oh,

God, the town had quarantined the dogs, but nobody had thought about the cats.

Elena's mind was working at top speed, but it wasn't helping her. It was only flashing pictures of what a cat could do with curved claws and needle-sharp teeth. And Margaret just lay there breathing softly, oblivious to any danger.

The fur on Snowball's back was rising, her tail swelling like a bottle brush. Her ears flattened and she opened her mouth in a silent hiss. Her eyes were fixed on Margaret's face just the way Chelsea's had been on Doug Carson's.

"No!" Elena looked around desperately for something to throw at the window, something to make noise. She couldn't get any closer; the outer branches of the tree wouldn't support her weight. "Margaret, wake up!"

But the snow, settling like a blanket around her, seemed to deaden the words into nothingness. A low, discordant wail was started in Snowball's throat as it flicked its eyes toward the window and then back to Margaret's face.

"Margaret, wake up!" Elena shouted. Then, just as the kitten pulled back a curved paw, she threw herself at the window.

She never knew, later, how she managed to hang on. There was no room to kneel on the sill, but her fingernails sank into the soft old wood of the casing, and the toe of one boot jammed into a foothold below. She banged against the window with her body weight, shouting.

"Get away from her! Wake up, Margaret!"

Margaret's eyes flew open and she sat up, throwing Snowball backward. The kitten's claws caught in the eyelet bedspread as it scrambled to right itself. Elena shouted again.

"Margaret, get off the bed! Open the window, quick!"

Margaret's four-year-old face was full of sleepy surprise, but no fear. She got up and stumbled toward the window while Elena gritted her teeth.

"That's it. Good girl . . . now say, 'Come in.' Quick, say it!"

"Come in," Margaret said obediently, blinking and stepping back.

The kitten sprang out as Elena fell in. She made a grab for it, but it was too fast. Once outside it glided across the maple branches with taunting ease and leaped down into the snow, disappearing.

A small hand was tugging at Elena's

sweater. "You came back!" Margaret said, hugging Elena's hips. "I missed you."

"Oh, Margaret, I missed *you*—" Elena began, and then froze. Aunt Judith's voice sounded from the top of the stairs.

"Margaret, are you awake? What's going on in there?"

Elena had only an instant to make her decision. "Don't tell her I'm here," she whispered, dropping to her knees. "It's a secret; do you understand? Say you let the kitty out, but don't tell her I'm here." There wasn't time for any more; Elena dived under the bed and prayed.

From under the dust ruffle, she watched Aunt Judith's stocking feet come into the room. She pressed her face into the floorboards, not breathing.

"Margaret! What are you doing up? Come on, let's get you back in bed," Aunt Judith's voice said, and then the bed creaked with Margaret's weight and Elena heard the noises of Aunt Judith's fussing with the covers. "Your hands are freezing. What on earth is the window doing open?"

"I opened it and Snowball went out," Margaret said. Elena let out her breath.

"And now there's snow all over the floor. I

can't believe this. . . . Don't you open it up again, do you hear me?" A little more bustling and the stocking feet went out again. The door shut.

Elena squirmed out.

"Good girl," she whispered as Margaret sat up. "I'm proud of you. Now tomorrow you tell Aunt Judith that you have to give your kitty away. Tell her it scared you. I know you don't want to"—she put up a hand to stop the wail that was gathering on Margaret's lips —"but you have to. Because I'm telling you that kitty will hurt you if you keep it. You don't want to get hurt, do you?"

"No," said Margaret, her blue eyes filling. "But—"

"And you don't want the kitty to hurt Aunt Judith, either, do you? You tell Aunt Judith you can't have a kitten or a puppy or even a bird until—well, for a while. Don't tell her that I said so; that's still our secret. Tell her you're scared because of what happened with the dogs at church." It was better, Elena reasoned grimly, to give the little girl nightmares than to have a nightmare play out in this bedroom.

Margaret's mouth drooped sadly. "Okay."

"I'm sorry, sweetie." Elena sat down and hugged her. "But that's the way it has to be."

"You're cold," Margaret said. Then she looked up into Elena's face. "Are you an angel?"

"Uh . . . not exactly." Just the opposite, Elena thought ironically.

"Aunt Judith said you went to be with Mommy and Daddy. Did you see them yet?"

"I—it's sort of hard to explain, Margaret. I haven't seen them yet, no. And I'm not an angel, but I'm going to be like your guardian angel anyway, all right? I'll watch over you, even when you can't see me. Okay?"

"Okay." Margaret played with her fingers. "Does that mean you can't live here anymore?"

Elena looked around the pink-and-white bedroom, at the stuffed animals on the shelves and the little writing desk and the rocking horse that had once been hers in the corner. "That's what it means," she said softly.

"When they said you went to be with Mommy and Daddy, I said I wanted to go, too."

Elena blinked hard. "Oh, baby. It's not time for you to go, so you can't. And Aunt

Judith loves you very much, and she'd be lonely without you."

Margaret nodded, her eyelids drooping. But as Elena eased her down and pulled the bedspread over her, Margaret asked one more question. "But don't *you* love me?"

"Oh, of course I do. I love you so much—I never even knew how much until now. But I'll be all right, and Aunt Judith needs you more. And . . ." Elena had to take a breath to steady herself, and when she looked down she saw Margaret's eyes were shut, her breathing regular. She was asleep.

Oh, stupid, *stupid*, Elena thought, forging through the banked snow to the other side of Maple Street. She'd missed her chance to ask Margaret whether Robert had been at dinner. It was too late now.

Robert. Her eyes narrowed suddenly. At the church, Robert had been outside and then the dogs had gone mad. And tonight Margaret's kitten had gone feral—just a little while after Robert's car had pulled out of the driveway.

Robert has a lot to answer for, she thought.

But melancholy was pulling at her, tugging her thoughts away. Her mind kept returning to the bright house she'd just left, going over the things she'd never see again. All her clothes and knickknacks and jewelry—what would Aunt Judith do with them? I don't own anything anymore, she thought. I'm a pauper.

Elena?

With relief, Elena recognized the mental voice and the distinctive shadow at the end of the street. She hurried toward Stefan, who took his hands out of his jacket pockets and held hers to warm them.

"Meredith told me where you'd gone."

"I went home," Elena said. That was all she could say, but as she leaned against him for comfort, she knew that he understood.

"Let's find someplace we can sit down," he said, and stopped in frustration. All the places they used to go were either too dangerous or closed to Elena. The police still had Stefan's car.

Eventually they just went to the high school where they could sit under the overhang of a roof and watch the snow sift down. Elena told him what had happened in Margaret's room.

"I'm going to have Meredith and Bonnie spread it around town that cats can attack, too. People should know that. And I think somebody ought to be watching Robert," she concluded.

"We'll tail him," Stefan said, and she couldn't help smiling.

"It's funny how much more American you've gotten," she said. "I hadn't thought about it in a long time, but when you first came you were a lot more foreign. Now nobody would know you hadn't lived here all your life."

"We adapt quickly. We have to," Stefan said. "There are always new countries, new decades, new situations. You'll adapt, too."

"Will I?" Elena's eyes remained on the glitter of falling snowflakes. "I don't know. . . ."

"You'll learn, in time. If there is anything . . . good . . . about what we are, it's time. We have plenty of it, as much as we want. Forever."

" 'Joyous companions forever.' Isn't that what Katherine said to you and Damon?" Elena murmured.

She could feel Stefan's stiffening, his withdrawal. "She was talking about all three of us," he said. "I wasn't."

"Oh, Stefan, please don't, not now. I wasn't even thinking about Damon, only about forever. It scares me. Everything about this scares me, and sometimes I think I just want to go to sleep and never wake up again. . . ."

In the shelter of his arms she felt safer, and she found her new senses were just as amazing close up as they were at a distance. She could hear each separate pulse of Stefan's heart, and the rush of blood through his veins. And she could smell his own distinctive scent mingled with the scent of his jacket, and the snow, and the wool of his clothes.

"Please trust me," she whispered. "I know you're angry with Damon, but try to give him a chance. I think there's more to him than there seems to be. And I want his help in finding the Other Power, and that's *all* I want from him."

At that moment it was completely true. Elena wanted nothing to do with the hunter's life tonight; the darkness held no appeal for her. She wished she could be at home sitting in front of a fire.

But it was sweet just to be held like this, even if she and Stefan had to sit in the snow to do it. Stefan's breath was warm as he kissed the back of her neck, and she sensed no further withdrawal in Stefan's body.

No hunger, either, or at least not the kind she was used to sensing when they were close like this. Now that she was a hunter like he, the need was different, a need for togetherness rather than for sustenance. It didn't matter. They had lost something, but they had gained something, too. She *understood* Stefan in a way she never had before. And her understanding brought them closer, until their minds were touching, almost meshing with each other's. It wasn't the noisy chatter of mental voices; it was a deep and wordless communion. As if their spirits were united.

"I love you," Stefan said against her neck, and she held on tighter. She understood now why he'd been afraid to say it for so long. When the thought of tomorrow scared you sick, it was hard to make a commitment. Because you didn't want to drag someone else down with you.

Particularly someone you loved. "I love you, too," she made herself say and sat back, her peaceful mood broken. "And will you try to give Damon a chance, for my sake? Try to work with him?"

"I'll work with him, but I won't trust him. I can't. I know him too well."

"I sometimes wonder if anybody knows

him at all. All right, then, do what you can. Maybe we can ask him to follow Robert to-morrow."

"I followed Mrs. Flowers today." Stefan's lip quirked. "All afternoon and evening. And you know what she did?"

"What?"

"Three loads of wash—in an ancient machine that looked like it was going to explode any minute. No clothes dryer, just a wringer. It's all down in the basement. Then she went outside and filled about two dozen bird feeders. Then back to the basement to wipe off jars of preserves. She spends most of her time down there. She talks to herself."

"Just like a dotty old lady," said Elena. "All right; maybe Meredith's wrong and that's all she is." She noticed his change of expression at Meredith's name and added, "What?"

"Well, Meredith may have some explaining to do herself. I didn't ask her about it; I thought maybe it was better coming from you. But she went to talk to Alaric Saltzman after school today. And she didn't want anyone to know where she was going."

Disquiet uncoiled in Elena's middle. "So what?"

"So she lied about it afterward—or at least

she evaded the issue. I tried to probe her mind, but my Powers are just about burnt out. And she's strong-willed."

"And you had no right! Stefan, listen to me. Meredith would never do anything to hurt us or betray us. Whatever she's keeping from us—"

"So you do admit that she's hiding something."

"Yes," Elena said reluctantly. "But it's nothing that will hurt us, I'm sure. Meredith has been my friend since the first grade. . . ." Without knowing it, Elena let the sentence slip away from her. She was thinking of another friend, one who'd been close to her since kindergarten. Caroline. Who last week had tried to destroy Stefan and humiliate Elena in front of the entire town.

And what was it Caroline's diary had said about Meredith? *Meredith doesn't do anything; she just watches. It's as if she can't act, she can only react to things. Besides, I've heard my parents talking about her family—no wonder she never mentions them.*

Elena's eyes left the snowy landscape to seek Stefan's waiting face. "It doesn't matter," she said quietly. "I know Meredith, and I trust her. I'll trust her to the end."

"I hope she's worthy of it, Elena," he said. "I really do."

Ten

December 12, Thursday morning
Dear Diary,

So after a week of work, what have we accomplished?

Well, between us we've managed to follow our three suspects just about continuously for the last six or seven days. Results: reports on Robert's movements for the last week, which he spent acting like any normal businessman. Reports on Alaric, who hasn't been doing anything unusual for a history teacher. Reports on Mrs. Flowers, who apparently spends most of her time in the basement. But we haven't really learned anything.

Stefan says that Alaric met with the principal a couple times, but he couldn't get close enough to hear what they were talking about.

Meredith and Bonnie spread the news about other pets besides dogs being dangerous. They didn't need to work very hard at it; it seems as if everybody in town is on the verge of hysteria already. Since then there've been several other animal attacks reported, but it's hard to know which ones to take seriously. Some kids were teasing a squirrel and it bit them. The Massases' pet rabbit scratched their littlest boy. Old Mrs. Coomber saw copperhead snakes in her yard, when all the snakes should be hibernating.

The only one I'm sure about is the attack on the vet who was keeping the dogs in quarantine. A bunch of them bit him and most of them escaped from the holding pens. After that they just disappeared. People are saying good riddance and hoping they'll starve in the woods, but I wonder.

And it's been snowing all the time. Not storming but not stopping, either. I've never seen so much snow.

Stefan's worried about the dance tomorrow night.

Which brings us back to: what have we learned so far? What do we know? None of our suspects were anywhere near the Massases' or Mrs. Coomber's or the vet's when the attacks happened. We're no closer to finding the Other Power than we were when we started.

Alaric's little get-together is tonight. Meredith thinks we should go to it. I don't know what else there is to do.

Damon stretched out his long legs and spoke lazily, looking around the barn. "No, I don't think it's dangerous, particularly. But I don't see what you expect to accomplish."

"Neither do I, exactly," Elena admitted. "But I don't have any better ideas. Do you?"

"What, you mean about other ways to spend the time? Yes, I do. Do you want me to tell you about them?" Elena waved him to silence and he subsided.

"I mean about useful things we can do at this point. Robert's out of town, Mrs. Flowers is down—"

"In the basement," chorused several voices.

"And we're all just sitting here. *Does* anybody have a better idea?"

Meredith broke the silence. "If you're worried about its being dangerous for me and Bonnie, why don't you *all* come? I don't mean you have to show yourselves. You could come and hide in the attic. Then if anything happened, we could scream for help and you would hear us."

"I don't see why anybody's going to be

screaming," said Bonnie. "Nothing's going to happen there."

"Well, maybe not, but it doesn't hurt to be safe," Meredith said. "What do you think?"

Elena nodded slowly. "It makes sense." She looked around for objections, but Stefan just shrugged, and Damon murmured something that made Bonnie laugh.

"All right, then, it's decided. Let's go."

The inevitable snow greeted them as they stepped outside the barn.

"Bonnie and I can go in my car," Meredith said. "And you three—"

"Oh, we'll find our own way," Damon said with his wolfish smile. Meredith nodded, not impressed. Funny, Elena thought as the other girls walked away; Meredith never *was* impressed with Damon. His charm seemed to have no effect on her.

She was about to mention that she was hungry when Stefan turned to Damon.

"Are you willing to stay with Elena the entire time you're over there? Every minute?" he said.

"Try and stop me," Damon said cheerfully. He dropped the smile. "Why?"

"Because if you are, the two of you can go

over alone, and I'll meet you later. I've got something to do, but it won't take long."

Elena felt a wave of warmth. He was trying to trust his brother. She smiled at Stefan in approval as he drew her aside.

"What is it?"

"I got a note from Caroline today. She asked if I would meet her at the school before Alaric's party. She said she wanted to apologize."

Elena opened her mouth to make a sharp remark, and then shut it again. From what she'd heard, Caroline was a sorry sight these days. And maybe it would make Stefan feel better to talk to her.

"Well, *you* don't have anything to apologize for," she told him. "Everything that happened to her was her own fault. You don't think she's dangerous at all?"

"No; I've got that much of my Powers left anyway. She's all right. I'll meet her, and she and I can go to Alaric's together."

"Be careful," Elena said as he started off into the snow.

The attic was as she remembered it, dark and dusty and full of mysterious oilcloth-covered shapes. Damon, who had come in more conventionally through the front door, had had to take the shutters off to let her in through the window. After that they sat side by side on the old mattress and listened to the voices that came up through the ducts.

"I could think of more romantic settings," Damon murmured, fastidiously pulling a cobweb off his sleeve. "Are you sure you wouldn't rather—"

"Yes," said Elena. "Now hush."

It was like a game, listening to the bits and pieces of conversations and trying to put them together, trying to match each voice to a face.

"And then I said, I don't care how long you've had the parakeet; get rid of it or I'm going to the Snow Dance with Mike Feldman. And he said—"

"—rumor going around that Mr. Tanner's grave was dug up last night—"

"—you hear that everybody but Caroline has dropped out of the snow queen competition? Don't you think—"

"—dead, but I'm telling you I *saw* her. And no, I wasn't dreaming; she was wearing a sort of silvery dress and her hair was all golden and blowing—"

Elena raised her eyebrows at Damon, then

looked meaningfully down at her sensible black attire. He grinned.

"Romanticism," he said. "Myself, I like you in black."

"Well, you would, wouldn't you?" she murmured. It was strange how much more comfortable she felt with Damon these days. She sat quietly, letting the conversations drift around her, almost losing track of time. Then she caught a familiar voice, cross, and closer than the rest.

"Okay, okay, I'm *going*. Okay."

Elena and Damon exchanged a glance and rose to their feet as the handle on the attic door turned. Bonnie peered around the edge.

"Meredith told me to come up here. I don't know why. She's hogging Alaric and it's a rotten party. Achoo!"

She sat down on the mattress, and after a few minutes Elena sat back down beside her. She was beginning to wish that Stefan would get here. By the time the door opened again and Meredith came in, she was sure of it.

"Meredith, what's going on?"

"Nothing, or at least nothing to worry about. Where's Stefan?" Meredith's cheeks were unusually flushed, and there was an odd look about her eyes, as if she were holding something tightly under control.

"He's coming later—" Elena began, but Damon interrupted.

"Never mind where he is. Who's coming up the stairs?"

"What do you mean, 'who's coming up the stairs?'" said Bonnie, rising.

"Everybody just stay *calm*," Meredith said, taking up a position in front of the window as if guarding it. She didn't look overly calm herself, Elena thought. "All right," she called, and the door opened and Alaric Saltzman came in.

Damon's motion was so smooth that even Elena's eyes couldn't follow it; in one movement he caught Elena's wrist and pulled her behind him, at the same time moving to face Alaric directly. He ended in a predator's crouch, every muscle drawn taut and ready for the attack.

"Oh, don't," cried Bonnie wildly. She flung herself at Alaric, who had already begun to recoil a step from Damon. Alaric nearly lost his balance and groped behind himself for the door. His other hand was groping at his belt.

"Stop it! Stop it!" Meredith said. Elena saw

the shape beneath Alaric's jacket and realized it was a gun.

Again, she couldn't quite follow what happened next. Damon let go of her wrist and took hold of Alaric's. And then Alaric was sitting on the floor, wearing a dazed expression, and Damon was emptying the gun of cartridges, one by one.

"I *told* you that was stupid and you wouldn't need it," Meredith said. Elena realized she was holding the dark-haired girl by the arms. She must have done it to keep Meredith from interfering with Damon, but she didn't remember.

"These wood-tipped things are nasty; they might hurt somebody," Damon said, mildly chiding. He replaced one of the cartridges and snapped the clip back in, aiming thoughtfully at Alaric.

"Stop it," said Meredith intensely. She turned to Elena. "Make him stop, Elena; he's only doing more harm. Alaric won't hurt you; I promise. I've spent all week convincing him that *you* won't hurt *him*."

"And now I think my wrist is broken," Alaric said, rather calmly. His sandy hair was falling into his eyes in front.

"You've got no one but yourself to blame,"

Meredith returned bitterly. Bonnie, who had been clutching solicitously at Alaric's shoulders, looked up at the familiarity of Meredith's tone, and then backed away a few paces and sat down.

"I can't wait to hear the explanation for *this*," she said.

"Please trust me," Meredith said to Elena. Elena looked into the dark eyes. She did trust Meredith; she'd said so. And the words stirred another memory, her own voice asking for Stefan's trust. She nodded.

"Damon?" she said. He flipped the gun away casually and then smiled around at all of them, making it abundantly clear that he didn't need any such artificial weapons.

"Now if everybody will just listen, you'll all understand," Meredith said.

"Oh, I'm *sure*," Bonnie said.

Elena walked toward Alaric Saltzman. She wasn't afraid of him, but by the way he looked only at her, slowly, starting from the feet and then continuing up, he was afraid of her.

She stopped when she was a yard from where he sat on the ground and knelt there, looking into his face.

"Hello," she said.

He was still holding his wrist. "Hello," he said, and gulped.

Elena glanced back at Meredith and then looked at Alaric again. Yes, he was scared. And with his hair in his eyes that way, he looked young. Maybe four years older than Elena, maybe five. No more than that.

"We're not going to hurt you," she said.

"That's what I've been telling him," Meredith said quietly. "I explained that whatever he's seen before, whatever stories he's heard, you're different. I told him what you told me about Stefan, how he's been fighting his nature all those years. I told him about what you've been going through, Elena, and how you never asked for this."

But *why* did you tell him so much? Elena thought. She said to Alaric, "All right, you know about us. But all we know about you is that you're not a history teacher."

"He's a hunter," Damon said softly, menacingly. "A vampire hunter."

"*No*," said Alaric. "Or at least, not in the sense that you mean it." He seemed to come to some decision. "All right. From what I know of you three—" He broke off, looking around the dark room as if suddenly realizing something. "Where's Stefan?"

173

"He's coming. In fact, he should be here by now. He was going to stop by the school and bring Caroline," Elena said. She was unprepared for Alaric's reaction.

"Caroline Forbes?" he said sharply, sitting up. His voice sounded the way it had when she'd overheard him talking with Dr. Feinberg and the principal, hard-edged and decisive.

"Yes. She sent him a note today, said she wanted to apologize or something. She wanted to meet him at school before the party."

"He can't go. You've got to stop him." Alaric scrambled to his feet and repeated urgently, "You've got to stop him."

"He's gone already. Why? Why shouldn't he?" Elena demanded.

"Because I hypnotized Caroline two days ago. I'd tried it earlier with Tyler, with no luck. But Caroline's a good subject, and she remembered a little of what happened in the Quonset hut. And she identified Stefan Salvatore as the attacker."

The shocked silence lasted only a fraction of a second. Then Bonnie said, "But what can Caroline do? She can't hurt him—"

"Don't you understand? You're not just

dealing with high school students anymore," Alaric said. "It's gone too far. Caroline's father knows about it, and Tyler's father. They're concerned for the safety of the town—"

"Hush! Be quiet!" Elena was casting about with her mind, trying to pick up some hint of Stefan's presence. He's let himself get weak, she thought, with the part of her that was icy calm amid the whirling fear and panic. At last she sensed something, just a trace, but she thought it was Stefan. And it was in distress.

"Something's wrong," Damon confirmed, and she realized he must have been searching, too, with a mind much more powerful than hers. "Let's go."

"Wait, let's talk first. Don't just go jumping into this." But Alaric might as well have been talking to the wind, trying to rein in its destructive power with words. Damon was already at the window, and the next moment Elena let herself drop out, landing neatly by Damon in the snow. Alaric's voice followed them from above.

"We're coming, too. *Wait* for us there. Let me talk to them first. I can take care of it. . . ."

Elena scarcely heard him. Her mind was

burning with one purpose, one thought. To hurt the people who wanted to hurt Stefan. It's gone too far, all right, she thought. And now *I'm* going to go as far as it takes. If they dare to touch him . . . images flashed through her mind, too quickly to count, of what she would do to them. At another time, she might have been shocked at the rush of adrenaline, of excitement, that coursed up at the thoughts.

She could sense Damon's mind beside her as they raced over the snow; it was like a blaze of red light and fury. The fierceness inside Elena welcomed it, glad to feel it so near. But then something else occurred to her.

"I'm slowing you down," she said. She was scarcely out of breath, even from running through unbroken snow, and they were making extraordinary time. But nothing on two legs, or even four, could match the speed of a bird's wings. "Go on," she said. "Get there as fast as you can. I'll meet you."

She didn't stay to watch the blur and shudder of the air, or the swirling darkness that ended in the rush of beating wings. But she glanced up at the crow that soared up and she heard Damon's mental voice.

Good hunting, it said, and the winged black shape arrowed toward the school.

Good hunting, Elena thought after him, meaning it. She redoubled her speed, her mind fixed all the while on that glimmer of Stefan's presence.

Stefan lay on his back, wishing his vision wasn't so blurred or that he had more than a tentative hold on consciousness. The blur was partly pain and partly snow, but there was also a trickle of blood from the three-inch wound in his scalp.

He'd been stupid, of course, not to look around the school; if he had he would have seen the darkened cars parked on the other side. He'd been stupid to come here in the first place. And now he was going to pay for that stupidity.

If only he could collect his thoughts enough to call for help . . . but the weakness that had allowed these men to overcome him so easily prevented that, too. He'd scarcely fed since the night he'd attacked Tyler. That was ironic, somehow. His own guilt was responsible for the mess he was in.

I should never have tried to change my nature, he thought. Damon had it right after all.

Everyone's the same—Alaric, Caroline, everyone. Everyone will betray you. I should have hunted them all and enjoyed it.

He hoped Damon would take care of Elena. She'd be safe with him; Damon was strong and ruthless. Damon would teach her to survive. He was glad of that.

But something inside him was crying.

The crow's sharp eyes spotted the crossing shafts of headlight below and dropped. But Damon didn't need the confirmation of sight; he was homing in on the faint pulsation that was Stefan's life-force. Faint because Stefan was weak and because he'd all but given up.

You never learn, do you, brother? Damon thought to him. *I ought to just leave you where you are.* But even as he skimmed the ground, he was changing, taking a shape that would do more damage than a crow.

The black wolf leaped into the knot of men surrounding Stefan, aiming precisely for the one holding the sharpened cylinder of wood above Stefan's chest. The force of the blow knocked the man ten feet backward, and the stake went skittering across the grass. Damon restrained his impulse—all the stronger because it fit the instincts of the shape he was wearing—to lock his teeth in the man's throat. He twisted around and went back for the other men who were still standing.

His second rush scattered them, but one of them reached the edge of the light and turned, lifting something to his shoulder. Rifle, thought Damon. And probably loaded with the same specially treated bullets as Alaric's handgun had been. There was no way to reach the man before he could get a shot off. The wolf growled and crouched for a leap anyway. The man's fleshy face creased in a smile.

Quick as a striking snake, a white hand reached out of the darkness and knocked the rifle away. The man looked around frantically, bewildered, and the wolf let its jaws fall open in a grin. Elena had arrived.

Eleven

Elena watched Mr. Smallwood's rifle bounce across the grass. She enjoyed the expression on his face as he spun around, looking for what had grabbed it. And she felt the flare of Damon's approval from across the pool of light, fierce and hot like the pride of a wolf for its cub's first kill. But when she glimpsed Stefan lying on the ground, she forgot everything else. White fury took her breath away, and she started toward him.

"Everybody stop! Just stop everything, right where you are!"

The shout was borne toward them along with the sound of tires squealing. Alaric Saltzman's car nearly spun out as it turned into the staff parking lot and screeched to a halt, and Alaric leaped from the car almost before it stopped moving.

"What's going on here?" he demanded, striding toward the men.

At the shout, Elena had pulled back automatically into the shadows. Now, she looked at the men's faces as they turned toward him. Besides Mr. Smallwood, she recognized Mr. Forbes and Mr. Bennett, Vickie Bennett's father. The others must be the fathers of the other guys who'd been with Tyler in the Quonset hut, she thought.

It was one of the strangers who answered the question, in a drawl that couldn't quite hide the nervousness underneath. "Well now, we just got a little tired of waiting any longer. We decided to speed things up a bit."

The wolf growled, a low rumbling that rose to a chainsaw snarl. All the men flinched back, and Alaric's eyes showed white as he noticed the animal for the first time.

There was another sound, softer and continuous, coming from a figure huddled next to one of the cars. Caroline Forbes was whimpering over and over, "They said they just wanted to talk to him. They didn't tell me what they were going to do."

Alaric, with one eye on the wolf, gestured

182

toward her. "And you were going to let her see *this*? A young girl? Do you realize the psychological damage that could do?"

"What about the psychological damage when her throat gets ripped out?" Mr. Forbes returned, and there were shouts of agreement. "That's what *we're* worried about."

"Then you'd better worry about getting the right man," Alaric said. "Caroline," he added, turning toward the girl, "I want you to think, Caroline. We didn't get to finish your sessions. I know when we left off you thought you recognized Stefan. But, are you absolutely positive it was him? Could it have been somebody else, somebody who resembled him?"

Caroline straightened, bracing herself against the car and raising a tear-stained face. She looked at Stefan, who was just sitting up, and then at Alaric. "I . . ."

"Think, Caroline. You have to be absolutely certain. Is there someone else it could have been, like—"

"Like that guy who calls himself Damon Smith," came Meredith's voice. She was standing beside Alaric's car, a slim shadow. "You remember him, Caroline? He came to Alaric's first party. He looks like Stefan in some ways."

183

Tension held Elena in perfect suspension as Caroline stared, uncomprehending. Then, slowly, the auburn-haired girl began to nod.

"Yes . . . it could have been, I suppose. Everything happened so fast . . . but it could have been."

"And you really can't be sure which it was?" Alaric said.

"No . . . not absolutely sure."

"There," said Alaric. "I told you she needed more sessions, that we couldn't be certain of anything yet. She's still very confused." He was walking, carefully, toward Stefan. Elena realized that the wolf had withdrawn back into the shadows. She could see it, but the men probably couldn't.

Its disappearance made them more aggressive. "What are you talking about? Who is this Smith? I've never seen him."

"But your daughter Vickie probably has, Mr. Bennett," Alaric said. "That may come out in my next session with her. We'll talk about it tomorrow; it can wait that long. Right now I think I'd better take Stefan to a hospital." There was discomforted shifting among some of the men.

"Oh, certainly, and while we're waiting

anything could happen," began Mr. Smallwood. "Any time, anywhere—"

"So you're just going to take the law into your own hands, then?" Alaric said. His voice sharpened. "Whether you've got the right suspect or not. Where's your evidence this boy has supernatural powers? What's your proof? How much of a fight did he even put up?"

"There's a wolf around somewhere who put up plenty of fight," Mr. Smallwood said, red-faced. "Maybe they're in it together."

"I don't see any wolf. I saw a dog. Maybe one of the dogs that got out of quarantine. But what's that got to do with it? I'm telling you that in my professional opinion you've got the wrong man."

The men were wavering, but there was still some doubt in their faces. Meredith spoke up.

"I think you should know that there've been vampire attacks in this county before," she said. "A long time before Stefan came here. My grandfather was a victim. Maybe some of you have heard about that." She looked across at Caroline.

That was the end of it. Elena could see the men exchanging uneasy glances and backing toward their cars. Suddenly they all seemed eager to be somewhere else.

Mr. Smallwood was one who stayed behind to say, "You said we'd talk about this tomorrow, Saltzman. I want to hear what my son says the next time *he's* hypnotized."

Caroline's father collected her and got in his car fast, muttering something about this all being a mistake and nobody taking it too seriously.

As the last car pulled away, Elena ran to Stefan.

"Are you all right? Did they hurt you?"

He moved away from Alaric's supporting arm. "Somebody hit me from behind while I was talking to Caroline. I'll be all right—now." He shot a glance at Alaric. "Thanks. Why?"

"He's on our side," said Bonnie, joining them. "I told you. Oh, Stefan, are you really okay? I thought I was going to faint there for a minute. They weren't serious. I mean, they couldn't really have been *serious.* . . ."

"Serious or not, I don't think we should stay here," said Meredith. "Does Stefan really need a hospital?"

"No," Stefan said, as Elena anxiously examined the cut on his head. "I just need rest. Somewhere to sit down."

"I've got my keys. Let's go to the history room," Alaric said.

Bonnie was looking around the shadows apprehensively. "The wolf, too?" she said, and then jumped as a shadow coalesced and became Damon.

"What wolf?" he said. Stefan turned slightly, wincing.

"Thank you, too," he said unemotionally. But Stefan's eyes lingered on his brother with something like puzzlement as they walked to the school building.

In the hallway, Elena pulled him aside. "Stefan, *why* didn't you notice them coming up behind you? Why were you so weak?"

Stefan shook his head evasively, and she added, "When did you feed last? Stefan, *when*? You always make some excuse when I'm around. What are you trying to do to yourself?"

"I'm all right," he said. "Really, Elena. I'll hunt later."

"Do you *promise*?"

"I promise."

It didn't occur to Elena at the moment that

they hadn't agreed on what "later" meant. She allowed him to lead her on down the hall.

The history room looked different at night to Elena's eyes. There was a strange atmosphere about it, as if the lights were too bright. Just now all the students' desks were shoved out of the way, and five chairs were pulled up to Alaric's desk. Alaric, who'd just finished arranging the furniture, urged Stefan into his own padded chair.

"Okay, why don't the rest of you take a seat."

They just looked at him. After a moment Bonnie sank down into a chair, but Elena stood by Stefan, Damon continued to lounge halfway between the group and the door, and Meredith pushed some papers to the center of Alaric's desk and perched on the corner.

The teacher look faded from Alaric's eyes. "All right," he said and sat down in one of the students' chairs himself. "Well."

"Well," said Elena.

Everyone looked at everyone else. Elena picked up a piece of cotton from the first-aid kit she'd grabbed at the door and began dabbing Stefan's head with it.

"I think it's time for that explanation," she said.

"Right. Yes. Well, you all seemed to have guessed I'm not a history teacher. . . ."

"In the first five minutes," Stefan said. His voice was quiet and dangerous, and with a jolt Elena realized it reminded her of Damon's. "So what are you?"

Alaric made an apologetic gesture and said almost diffidently, "A psychologist. Not the couch kind," he added hastily as the rest of them exchanged looks. "I'm a researcher, an experimental psychologist. From Duke University. You know, where the ESP experiments were started."

"The ones where they make you guess what's on the card without looking at it?" Bonnie asked.

"Yes, well, it's gone a bit beyond that now, of course. Not that I wouldn't love to test you with Rhine cards, especially when you're in one of those trances." Alaric's face lit with scientific inquiry. Then he cleared his throat and went on. "But—ah—as I was saying. It started a couple of years ago when I did a paper on parapsychology. I wasn't trying to prove supernatural powers existed, I just wanted to study what their psychological effect is on the people who have them. Bonnie, here, is a case in point." Alaric's voice took on a lecturer's tone. "What does it do to her, mentally, emotionally, to have to deal with these powers?"

"It's awful," Bonnie interrupted vehemently. "I don't want them anymore. I *hate* them."

"Well, there you see," Alaric said. "You'd have made a great case study. My problem was that I couldn't find anybody with real psychic powers to examine. There were plenty of fakers, all right—crystal healers, dowsers, channelers, you name it. But I couldn't find anything genuine until I got a tip from a friend in the police department.

"There was this woman down in South Carolina who claimed she'd been bitten by a vampire, and since then she was having psychic nightmares. By that time I was so used to fakes I expected her to turn out to be one, too. But she wasn't, at least not about being bitten. I never could prove she was really psychic."

"How could you be sure she'd been bitten?" Elena asked.

"There was medical evidence. Traces of saliva in her wounds that were similar to human saliva—but not quite the same. It contained an anticoagulatory agent similar to that found in the saliva of leeches. . . ." Alaric caught himself and hurried on. "Anyway, I was sure. And that was how it started. Once I was convinced something had really happened to the woman, I started to look up other cases like hers. There weren't a lot of them, but they were out there. People who'd encountered vampires.

"I dropped all my other studies and concentrated on finding victims of vampires and examining them. And if I say so myself, I've become the foremost expert in the field," Alaric concluded modestly. "I've written a number of papers—"

"But you've never actually seen a vampire," Elena interrupted. "Until now, I mean. Is that right?"

"Well—no. Not in the flesh, as it were. But I've written monographs . . . and things." His voice trailed off.

Elena bit her lip. "What were you doing with the dogs?" she asked. "At the church, when you were waving your hands at them."

"Oh . . ." Alaric looked embarrassed. "I've picked up a few things here and there, you know. That was a spell an old mountain man showed me for fending off evil. I thought it might work."

"You've got a lot to learn," said Damon.

"Obviously," Alaric said stiffly. Then he grimaced. "Actually, I figured that out right after I got here. Your principal, Brian Newcastle, had heard of me. He knew about the studies I do. When Tanner was killed and Dr. Feinberg found no blood in the body and lacerations made by teeth in the neck . . . well, they gave me a call. I thought it could be a big break for me—a case with the vampire still in the area. The only problem was that once I got here I realized they expected *me* to take care of the vampire. They didn't know I'd dealt only with the victims before. And . . . well, maybe I was in over my head. But I did my best to justify their confidence—"

"You faked it," Elena accused. "That was what you were doing when I heard you talking to them at your house about finding our supposed lair and all that. You were just winging it."

"Well, not *completely*," Alaric said. "Theoretically, I *am* an expert." Then he did a double take. "What do you mean, when you heard me talking to them?"

"While you were out searching for a lair, she was sleeping in your attic," Damon informed him dryly. Alaric opened his mouth and then shut it again.

"What I'd like to know is how Meredith comes into all this," Stefan said. He wasn't smiling.

Meredith, who had been gazing thoughtfully at the jumble of papers on Alaric's desk during all this, looked up. She spoke evenly, without emotion.

"I recognized him, you see. I couldn't remember where I'd seen him at first, because it was almost three years ago. Then I realized it was at Granddad's hospital. What I told those men was the truth, Stefan. My grandfather was attacked by a vampire."

There was a little silence and then Meredith went on. "It happened a long time ago, before I was born. He wasn't badly hurt by it, but he never really got well. He became . . . well, sort of like Vickie, only more violent. It got so that they were afraid he'd harm himself, or somebody else. So they took him to a hospital, a place he'd be safe."

"A mental institution," Elena said. She felt a pang of sympathy for the dark-haired girl. "Oh, Meredith. But why didn't you say anything? You could have told us."

"I know. I could have . . . but I couldn't.

The family's kept it a secret so long—or tried anyway. From what Caroline wrote in her diary, she'd obviously heard. The thing is, nobody ever believed Granddad's stories about the vampire. They just thought it was another of his delusions, and he had a lot of them. Even I didn't believe them . . . until Stefan came. And then—I don't know, my mind started to put little things together. But I didn't really *believe* what I was thinking until you came back, Elena."

"I'm surprised you didn't hate me," Elena said softly.

"How could I? I *know* you, and I know Stefan. I know you're not evil." Meredith didn't glance at Damon; he might as well not have been present for all the acknowledgment she gave him. "But when I remembered seeing Alaric talking to Granddad at the hospital I knew *he* wasn't, either. I just didn't know exactly how to get all of you together to prove it."

"I didn't recognize you, either," Alaric said. "The old man had a different name—he's your mother's father, right? And I may have seen you hanging around the waiting room sometime, but you were just a kid with skinny legs then. You've changed," he added appreciatively.

Bonnie coughed, a pointed sound.

Elena was trying to arrange things in her mind. "So what were those men doing out there with a stake if you didn't tell them to be?"

"I had to ask Caroline's parents for permission to hypnotize her, of course. And I reported what I found to them. But if you're thinking I had anything to do with what happened tonight, you're wrong. I didn't even know about it."

"I've told him about what we've been doing, how we've been looking for the Other Power," Meredith said. "And he wants to help."

"I said I *might* help," Alaric said cautiously.

"Wrong," said Stefan. "You're either with us or against us. I'm grateful for what you did out there, talking to those men, but the fact remains that you started a lot of this trouble in the first place. Now you have to decide: are you on our side—or theirs?"

Alaric looked around at each of them, at Meredith's steady gaze and Bonnie's raised eyebrows, at Elena kneeling on the floor and at Stefan's already-healing scalp. Then he turned to glance at Damon, who was leaning against the wall, dark and saturnine. "I'll help," he said at last. "Hell, it's the ultimate case study."

"All right, then," Elena said. "You're in. Now, what about Mr. Smallwood tomorrow? What if he wants you to hypnotize Tyler again?"

"I'll stall him," Alaric said. "It won't work forever, but it'll buy some time. I'll tell him I've got to help with the dance—"

"Wait," said Stefan. "There shouldn't *be* a dance, not if there's any way to prevent it. You're on good terms with the principal; you can talk to the school board. Make them cancel it."

Alaric looked startled. "You think something's going to happen?"

"Yes," Stefan said. "Not just because of what's happened at the other public functions, but because something's building up. It's been building up all week; I can feel it."

"So can I," Elena said. She hadn't realized it until that moment, but the tension she felt, the sense of urgency, was not just from inside her. It was outside, all around. It thickened the air. "Something's going to happen, Alaric."

Alaric let out his breath in a soft whistle. "Well, I can try to convince them, but—I don't know. Your principal is dead set on keeping everything looking normal. And it isn't as if I can give any rational explanation for wanting to shut it down."

"Try *hard*," Elena said.

"I will. And meanwhile, maybe you should think about protecting yourself. If what Meredith says is right, then most of the attacks have been on you and people close to you. *Your* boyfriend got dropped in a well; your car got chased into the river; your memorial service was broken up. Meredith says even your little sister was threatened. If something's going to happen tomorrow, you might want to leave town."

It was Elena's turn to be startled. She had never thought of the attacks in that way, but it was true. She heard Stefan's indrawn breath and felt his fingers tighten on hers.

"He's right," Stefan said. "You should leave, Elena. I can stay here until—"

"*No.* I'm not going without you. And," Elena continued, slowly, thinking it out, "I'm not going *anywhere* until we find the Other Power and stop it." She looked up at him earnestly, speaking quickly now. "Oh, Stefan, don't you see, nobody else even has a chance against it. Mr. Smallwood and his friends don't have a clue. Alaric thinks you can fight it by waving your hands at it. *None* of them know what they're up against. We're the only ones who can help."

She could see the resistance in Stefan's eyes and feel it in the tenor of his muscles. But as she kept on looking straight at him, she saw his objections fall one by one. For the simple reason that it was the truth, and Stefan hated lying.

"All right," he said at last, painfully. "But as soon as this is all over, we're leaving. I'm not having you stay in a town where vigilantes run around with stakes."

"Yes." Elena returned the pressure of his fingers with hers. "Once this is all over, we'll go."

Stefan turned to Alaric. "And if there's no way to talk them out of having the dance tomorrow, I think we should keep an eye on it. If something does happen, we may be able to stop it before it gets out of hand."

"That's a good idea," Alaric said, perking up. "We could meet tomorrow after dark here in the history room. Nobody comes here. We could keep up a watch all night."

Elena tilted a doubtful eye toward Bonnie. "Well . . . it would mean missing the dance itself—for those of us who could have gone, I mean."

Bonnie drew herself up. "Oh, who cares about missing a *dance?*" she said indignantly. "What on earth does a *dance* matter to anyone?"

"Right," said Stefan gravely. "Then it's settled." A spasm of pain seemed to overtake him and he winced, looking down. Elena was immediately concerned.

"You need to get home and rest," she said. "Alaric, can you drive us? It's not that far."

Stefan protested that he was perfectly able to walk, but in the end he gave in. At the boardinghouse, after Stefan and Damon had gotten out of the car, Elena leaned in Alaric's window for one last question. It had been gnawing at her mind ever since Alaric had told them his story.

"About those people who'd encountered vampires," she said. "Just what were the psychological effects? I mean, did they all go crazy or have nightmares? Were any of them okay?"

"It depends on the individual," Alaric said. "And with how many contacts they'd had, and what kind of contacts they were. But mostly just with the personality of the victim, with how well the individual mind can cope."

Elena nodded, and said nothing until the lights of Alaric's car had been swallowed by the snowy air. Then she turned to Stefan.

"Matt."

Twelve

Stefan looked at Elena, snow crystals dusting his dark hair. "What about Matt?"

"I remember—something. It's not clear. But that first night, when I wasn't myself— did I see Matt then? Did I—?"

Fear and a sick sense of dismay swelled her throat and cut her words off. But she didn't need to finish, and Stefan didn't need to answer. She saw it in his eyes.

"It was the only way, Elena," he said then. "You would have died without human blood. Would you rather have attacked somebody unwilling, hurt them, maybe killed them? The need can drive you to that. Is that what you would have wanted?"

"*No,*" Elena said violently. "But did it have

to be Matt? Oh, don't answer that; I can't think of anybody else, either." She took a shaky breath. "But now I'm worried about him, Stefan. I haven't seen him since that night. Is he okay? What has he said to you?"

"Not much," said Stefan, looking away. " 'Leave me alone' was about the gist of it. He also denied that anything happened that night, and said that you were dead."

"Sounds like one of those individuals who can't cope," Damon commented.

"Oh, shut up!" said Elena. "You keep out of this, and while you're at it, you might think about poor Vickie Bennett. How d'you think *she's* coping these days?"

"It might help if I knew who this Vickie Bennett is. You keep talking about her, but I've never met the girl."

"Yes, you have. Don't play games with me, Damon—the cemetery, remember? The ruined church? The girl you left wandering around there in her slip?"

"Sorry, no. And I usually *do* remember girls I leave wandering in their slips."

"I suppose Stefan did it, then," Elena said sarcastically.

Anger flashed to the surface of Damon's eyes, covered quickly with a disturbing smile.

"Maybe he did. Maybe *you* did. It's all the same to me, except that I'm getting a little tired of accusations. And now—"

"Wait," said Stefan, with surprising mildness. "Don't go yet. We should talk—"

"I'm afraid I have a previous engagement." There was a flurry of wings, and Stefan and Elena were alone.

Elena put a knuckle to her lips. "Damn. I didn't mean to make him angry. After he was really almost civilized all evening."

"Never mind," said Stefan. "He likes to be angry. What were you saying about Matt?"

Elena saw the weariness in Stefan's face and put an arm around him. "We won't talk about it now, but I think tomorrow maybe we should go see him. To tell him . . ." Elena lifted her other hand helplessly. She didn't know what she wanted to tell Matt; she only knew that she needed to do *something.*

"I think," said Stefan slowly, "that *you* had better go see him. I tried to talk to him, but he didn't want to listen to me. I can understand that, but maybe you'll do better. And I think," he paused and then went on resolutely, "I think you'd do better alone with him. You could go now."

Elena looked at him hard. "Are you sure?"

"Yes."

"But—will you be all right? I should stay with you—"

"I'll be fine, Elena," Stefan said gently. "Go on."

Elena hesitated, then nodded. "I won't be long," she promised him.

Unseen, Elena slipped around the side of the frame house with the peeling paint and the crooked mailbox labeled *Honeycutt*. Matt's window was unlocked. Careless boy, she thought reprovingly. Don't you know something might come creeping in? She eased it open, but of course that was as far as she could go. An invisible barrier that felt like a soft wall of thickened air blocked her way.

"Matt," she whispered. The room was dark, but she could see a vague shape on the bed. A digital clock with pale green numbers showed that it was 12:15. "Matt," she whispered again.

The figure stirred. "Uh?"

"Matt, I don't want to frighten you." She made her voice soothing, trying to wake him gently rather than startle him out of his wits. "But it's me, Elena, and I wanted to talk.

Only you've got to ask me in first. Can you ask me in?"

"Uh. C'mon in." Elena was amazed at the lack of surprise in his voice. It was only after she'd gotten over the sill that she realized he was still asleep.

"Matt. *Matt*," she whispered, afraid to go too close. The room was stifling and overheated, the radiator going full blast. She could see a bare foot sticking out of the mound of blankets on the bed and blond hair at the top.

"Matt?" Tentatively, she leaned over and touched him.

That got a response. With an explosive grunt, Matt sat bolt upright, whipping around. When his eyes met hers, they were wide and staring.

Elena found herself trying to look small and harmless, nonthreatening. She backed away against the wall. "I didn't mean to frighten you. I know it's a shock. But will you talk to me?"

He simply went on staring at her. His yellow hair was sweaty and ruffled up like wet chicken feathers. She could see his pulse pounding in his bare neck. She was afraid he was going to get up and dash out of the room.

Then his shoulders relaxed, slumping, and he slowly shut his eyes. He was breathing deeply but raggedly. "Elena."

"Yes," she whispered.

"You're dead."

"No. I'm here."

"Dead people don't come back. My dad didn't come back."

"I didn't really die. I just changed." Matt's eyes were still shut in repudiation, and Elena felt a cold wave of hopelessness wash over her. "But you wish I had died, don't you? I'll leave now," she whispered.

Matt's face cracked and he started to cry.

"No. Oh, no. Oh, don't, Matt, please." She found herself cradling him, fighting not to cry herself. "Matt, I'm sorry; I shouldn't even have come here."

"Don't leave," he sobbed. "Don't go away."

"I won't." Elena lost the fight, and tears fell onto Matt's damp hair. "I didn't mean to hurt you, ever," she said. "Not *ever*, Matt. All those times, all those things I did—I never wanted to hurt you. Truly . . ." Then she stopped talking and just held him.

After a while his breathing quieted and he

sat back, swiping his face with a fistful of sheet. His eyes avoided hers. There was a look on his face, not just of embarrassment, but of distrust, as if he were bracing himself for something he dreaded.

"Okay, so you're here. You're alive," he said roughly. "So what do you want?"

Elena was dumbfounded.

"Come on, there must be something. What is it?"

New tears welled up, but Elena gulped them back. "I guess I deserve that. I *know* I do. But for once, Matt, I want absolutely nothing. I came to apologize, to say that I'm sorry for using you—not just that one night, but always. I care about you, and I care if you hurt. I thought maybe I could make things better." After a heavy silence, she added, "I guess I *will* leave now."

"No, wait. Wait a second." Matt scrubbed at his face with the sheet again. "Listen. That was stupid, and I'm a jerk—"

"That was the truth and you're a gentleman. Or you'd've told me to go take a hike a long time ago."

"No, I'm a stupid jerk. I should be banging my head against the wall with joy because you're not dead. I will in a minute. Listen." He grabbed her wrist and Elena looked at it in mild surprise. "I don't care if you're the Creature from the Black Lagoon, It, Godzilla and Frankenstein all rolled up into one. I just—"

"Matt." Panicked, Elena put her free hand over his mouth.

"I know. You're engaged to the guy in the black cape. Don't worry; I remember him. I even like him, though God knows why." Matt took a breath and seemed to calm down. "Look, I don't know if Stefan told you. He said a bunch of stuff to me—about being evil, about not being sorry for what he did to Tyler. You know what I'm talking about?"

Elena shut her eyes. "He's scarcely eaten since that night. I think he's hunted once. Tonight he almost got himself killed because he's so weak."

Matt nodded. "So it was your basic crap. I should have known."

"Well, it is and it isn't. The need is strong, stronger than you can imagine." It was dawning on Elena that *she* hadn't fed today and that she'd been hungry before they'd set out for Alaric's. "In fact—Matt, I'd better go. Just one thing—if there's a dance tomorrow night, don't go. Something's going to happen then, something bad. We're going to try to guard it, but I don't know what we can do."

"Who's 'we'?" Matt said sharply.

"Stefan and Damon—I think Damon—and me. And Meredith and Bonnie . . . and Alaric Saltzman. Don't ask about Alaric. It's a long story."

"But what are you guarding *against*?"

"I forgot; you don't know. *That's* a long story, too, but . . . well, the short answer is, whatever killed me. Whatever made those dogs attack people at my memorial service. It's something bad, Matt, that's been around Fell's Church for a while now. And we're going to try to stop it from doing anything tomorrow night." She tried not to squirm. "Look, I'm sorry, but I really should leave." Her eyes drifted, despite herself, to the broad blue vein in his neck.

When she managed to tear her gaze away and look at his face, she saw shock giving way to sudden understanding. Then to something incredible: acceptance. "It's okay," Matt said.

She wasn't sure she'd heard correctly. "Matt?"

"I said, it's okay. It didn't hurt me before."

"No. No, Matt, really. I didn't *come* here for that—"

"I know. That's why I want to. I want to give you something you *didn't* ask for." After a moment he said, "For old friends' sake."

Stefan, Elena was thinking. But Stefan had told her to come, and come alone. Stefan had known, she realized. And it was all right. It was his gift to Matt—and to her.

But I'm coming back to *you*, Stefan, she thought.

As she leaned toward him, Matt said, "I'm going to come and help you tomorrow, you know. Even if I'm not invited."

Then her lips touched his throat.

December 13, Friday
Dear Diary,

Tonight's the night.

I know I've written that before, or thought it at least. But tonight is the night, the big one, when everything is going to happen. This is it.

Stefan feels it, too. He came back from school today to tell me that the dance is still on—Mr. Newcastle didn't want to cause a panic by canceling it or something. What they're going to do is have "security" outside, which means the police, I guess. And maybe Mr. Smallwood and some of his friends with rifles. Whatever's going to happen, I don't think they can stop it.

I don't know if we can, either.

It's been snowing all day. The pass is blocked, which means nothing gets in or out of town on wheels. Until the snowplow gets up there, which won't be until morning, which will be too late.

And the air has a funny feeling to it. Not just snow. It's as if something even colder than that is waiting. It's pulled back the way the ocean pulls back before a tidal wave. When it lets go . . .

I thought about my other diary today, the one under the floorboards of my bedroom closet. If I own anything anymore, I own that diary. I thought about getting it out, but I don't want to go home again. I don't think I could cope, and I know Aunt Judith couldn't if she saw me.

I'm surprised anybody's been able to cope. Meredith, Bonnie—especially Bonnie. Well, Meredith, too, considering what her family has been through. Matt.

They're good and loyal friends. It's funny, I used to think that without a whole galaxy of friends and admirers I wouldn't survive. Now I'm perfectly happy with three, thank you. Because they're real friends.

I didn't know how much I cared about them

before. Or about Margaret, or Aunt Judith even. And everybody at school . . . I know a few weeks ago I was saying that I didn't care if the entire population of Robert E. Lee dropped dead, but that isn't true. Tonight I'm going to do my best to protect them.

I know I'm jumping from subject to subject, but I'm just talking about things that are important to me. Kind of gathering them together in my mind. Just in case.

Well, it's time. Stefan is waiting. I'm going to finish this last line and then go.

I think we're going to win. I hope so.

We're going to try.

The history room was warm and brightly lit. On the other side of the school building, the cafeteria was even brighter, shining with Christmas lights and decorations. Upon arriving, Elena had scrutinized it from a cautious distance, watching the couples arrive for the dance and pass by the sheriff's officers at the door. Feeling Damon's silent presence behind her, she had pointed out a girl with long, light brown hair.

"Vickie Bennett," she said.

"I'll take your word for it," he replied.

Now, she looked around their makeshift

headquarters for the night. Alaric's desk had been cleared, and he was bent over a rough map of the school. Meredith leaned in beside him, her dark hair sweeping his sleeve. Matt and Bonnie were out mingling with the dancegoers in the parking lot, and Stefan and Damon were prowling the perimeter of the school grounds. They were going to take turns.

"You'd better stay inside," Alaric had told Elena. "All we need is for somebody to see you and start chasing you with a stake."

"I've been walking around town all week," Elena said, amused. "If I don't want to be seen, you don't see me." But she agreed to stay in the history room and coordinate.

It's like a castle, she thought as she watched Alaric plot out the positions of sheriff's officers and other men on the map. And we're defending it. Me and my loyal knights.

The round, flat-faced clock on the wall ticked the minutes by. Elena watched it as she let people in the door and let them out again. She poured hot coffee out of a Thermos for those who wanted it. She listened to the reports come in.

"Everything's quiet on the north side of the school."

"Caroline just got crowned snow queen. Big surprise."

"Some rowdy kids in the parking lot—the sheriff just rounded them up. . . ."

Midnight came and went.

"Maybe we were wrong," Stefan said an hour or so later. It was the first time they'd all been inside together since the beginning of the evening.

"Maybe it's happening somewhere else," said Bonnie, emptying out a boot and peering into it.

"There's no way to know where it's going to happen," Elena said firmly. "But we weren't wrong about it happening."

"Maybe," said Alaric thoughtfully, "there *is* a way. To find out where it's going to happen, I mean." As heads raised questioningly, he said, "We need a precognition."

All eyes turned to Bonnie.

"Oh, no," Bonnie said. "I'm through with all that. I *hate* it."

"It's a great gift—" began Alaric.

"It's a great big pain. Look, you don't understand. The ordinary predictions are bad enough. It seems like most of the time I'm finding out things I don't want to know. But getting taken over—that's *awful*. And after-

214

ward I don't even remember what I've said. It's horrible."

"Getting taken over?" Alaric repeated. "What's that?"

Bonnie sighed. "It's what happened to me in the church," she said patiently. "I can do other kinds of predictions, like divining with water or reading palms"—she glanced at Elena, and then away—"and stuff like that. But then there are times when—someone—takes me over and just uses me to talk for them. It's like having somebody else in my body."

"Like in the graveyard, when you said there was something there waiting for me," said Elena. "Or when you warned me not to go near the bridge. Or when you came to dinner and said that Death, my death, was in the house." She looked automatically around at Damon, who returned her gaze impassively. Still, that had been wrong, she thought. Damon hadn't been her death. So what had the prophecy meant? For just an instant something glimmered in her mind, but before she could get a grasp on it, Meredith interrupted.

"It's like another voice that speaks through Bonnie," Meredith explained to Alaric. "She even looks different. Maybe you weren't close enough in the church to see."

"But why didn't you tell me about this?" Alaric was excited. "This could be important. This—entity—whatever it is—could give us vital information. It could clear up the mystery of the Other Power, or at least give us a clue how to fight it."

Bonnie was shaking her head. "No. It isn't something I can just whistle up, and it doesn't answer questions. It just *happens* to me. And I hate it."

"You mean you can't think of anything that tends to set it off? Anything that's led to it happening before?"

Elena and Meredith, who knew very well what could set it off, looked at each other. Elena bit the inside of her cheek. It was Bonnie's choice. It had to be Bonnie's choice.

Bonnie, who was holding her head in her hands, shot a sideways glance through red curls at Elena. Then she shut her eyes and moaned.

"Candles," she said.

"What?"

"*Candles.* A candle flame might do it. I can't be sure, you understand; I'm not promising *anything*—"

"Somebody go ransack the science lab," said Alaric.

It was a scene reminiscent of the day Alaric had come to school, when he'd asked them all to put their chairs in a circle. Elena looked at the circle of faces lit eerily from below by the candle's flame. There was Matt, with his jaw set. Beside him, Meredith, her dark lashes throwing shadows upward. And Alaric, leaning forward in his eagerness. Then Damon, light and shadow dancing over the planes of his face. And Stefan, high cheekbones looking too sharply defined to Elena's eyes. And finally, Bonnie, looking fragile and pale even in the golden light of the candle.

We're connected, Elena thought, overcome by the same feeling that she'd had in the church, when she had taken Stefan's and Damon's hands. She remembered a thin white circle of wax floating in a dish of water. *We can do it if we stick together.*

"I'm just going to look into the candle," Bonnie said, her voice quivering slightly. "And not think of anything. I'm going to try to—leave myself open to it." She began to breathe deeply, gazing into the candle flame.

And then it happened, just as it had

before. Bonnie's face smoothed out, all expression draining away. Her eyes went blank as the stone cherub's in the graveyard.

She didn't say a word.

That was when Elena realized they hadn't agreed on what to ask. She groped through her mind to find a question before Bonnie lost contact. "Where can we find the Other Power?" she said, just as Alaric blurted out, "Who are you?" Their voices mingled, their questions intertwining.

Bonnie's blank face turned, sweeping the circle with sightless eyes. Then the voice that wasn't Bonnie's voice said, "Come and see."

"Wait a minute," Matt said, as Bonnie stood up, still entranced, and made for the door. "Where's she going?"

Meredith grabbed for her coat. "Are we going with her?"

"Don't touch her!" said Alaric, jumping up as Bonnie went out the door.

Elena looked at Stefan, and then at Damon. With one accord, they followed, trailing Bonnie down the empty, echoing hall.

"Where are we going? Which question is she answering?" Matt demanded. Elena could only shake her head. Alaric was jogging to keep up with Bonnie's gliding pace.

She slowed down as they emerged into the snow, and to Elena's surprise, walked up to Alaric's car in the staff parking lot and stood beside it.

"We can't all fit; I'll follow with Matt," Meredith said swiftly. Elena, her skin chilled with apprehension as well as cold air, got in the back of Alaric's car when he opened it for her, with Damon and Stefan on either side. Bonnie sat up front. She was looking straight ahead, and she didn't speak. But as Alaric pulled out of the parking lot, she lifted one white hand and pointed. Right on Lee Street and then left on Arbor Green. Straight out toward Elena's house and then right on Thunderbird. Heading toward Old Creek Road.

It was then that Elena realized where they were going.

They took the other bridge to the cemetery, the one everyone always called "the new bridge" to distinguish it from Wickery Bridge, which was now gone. They were approaching from the gate side, the side Tyler had driven up when he took Elena to the ruined church.

Alaric's car stopped just where Tyler's had stopped. Meredith pulled up behind them.

With a terrible sense of déjà vu, Elena

made the trek up the hill and through the gate, following Bonnie to where the ruined church stood with its belfry pointing like a finger to the stormy sky. At the empty hole that had once been the doorway, she balked.

"Where are you taking us?" she said. "*Listen* to me. Will you just tell us which question you're answering?"

"Come and see."

Helplessly, Elena looked at the others. Then she stepped over the threshold. Bonnie walked slowly to the white marble tomb, and stopped.

Elena looked at it, and then at Bonnie's ghostly face. Every hair on her arms and the back of her neck was standing up. "Oh, no . . ." she whispered. "Not that."

"Elena, what are you talking about?" Meredith said.

Dizzy, Elena looked down at the marble countenances of Thomas and Honoria Fell, lying on the stone lid of their tomb. "This thing opens," she whispered.

Thirteen

"You think we're supposed to—look inside?" Matt said.

"I don't know," Elena said miserably. She didn't want to see what was inside that tomb now any more than she had when Tyler had suggested opening it to vandalize it. "Maybe we won't be able to *get* it open," she added. "Tyler and Dick couldn't. It started to slide only when I leaned on it."

"Lean on it now; maybe there's some sort of hidden spring mechanism," Alaric suggested, and when Elena did, with no results, he said, "All right, let's all get a grip, and brace ourselves—like this. Come on, now—"

From his crouch, he looked up at Damon, who was standing motionless next to the tomb, looking faintly amused. "Excuse me," Damon said, and Alaric stepped back, frowning. Damon and Stefan each gripped an end of the stone lid and lifted.

The lid came away, making a grinding sound as Damon and Stefan slid it to the ground on one side of the tomb.

Elena couldn't bring herself to move closer.

Instead, fighting nausea, she concentrated on Stefan's expression. It would tell her what was to be found in there. Pictures crashed through her mind, of parchment-colored mummified bodies, of rotting corpses, of grinning skulls. If Stefan looked horrified or sickened, disgusted . . .

But as Stefan looked into the open tomb, his face registered only disconcerted surprise.

Elena couldn't stand it any longer. "What is it?"

He gave her a crooked smile and said with a glance at Bonnie, "Come and see."

Elena inched up to the tomb and looked down. Then her head flew up, and she regarded Stefan in astonishment.

"What is it?"

"I don't know," he replied. He turned to Meredith and Alaric. "Does either of you have a flashlight? Or some rope?"

After a look inside the stone box, they both headed for their cars. Elena remained where she was, staring down, straining her night vision. She still couldn't believe it.

The tomb was not a tomb, but a doorway.

Now she understood why she had felt a cold wind blow from it when it had shifted beneath her hand that night. She was looking down into a kind of vault or cellar in the ground. She could see only one wall, the one that dropped straight down below her, and that one had iron rungs driven into the stone, like a ladder.

"Here you go," Meredith said to Stefan, returning. "Alaric's got a flashlight, and here's mine. And here's the rope Elena put in my car when we went looking for you."

The narrow beam of Meredith's flashlight swept the dark room below. "I can't see very far inside, but it looks empty," Stefan said. "I'll go down first."

"Go *down?*" said Matt. "Look, are you sure we're *supposed* to go down? Bonnie, how about it?"

Bonnie hadn't moved. She was still standing there with that utterly abstracted expression on her face, as if she saw nothing around her. Without a word, she swung a leg over the edge of the tomb, twisted, and began to descend.

"Whoa," said Stefan. He tucked the flashlight in his jacket pocket, put a hand on the tomb's foot, and jumped.

Elena had no time to enjoy Alaric's expression; she leaned down and shouted, "Are you okay?"

"Fine." The flashlight winked at her from below. "Bonnie will be all right, too. The rungs go all the way down. Better bring the rope anyway."

Elena looked at Matt, who was closest. His blue eyes met hers with helplessness and a certain resignation, and he nodded. She took a deep breath and put a hand on the foot of the tomb as Stefan had. Another hand suddenly clamped on her wrist.

"I've just thought of something," Meredith said grimly. "What if Bonnie's entity *is* the Other Power?"

"I thought of that a long time ago," Elena said. She patted Meredith's hand, pried it off, and jumped.

She stood up into Stefan's supporting arm and looked around. "My God . . ."

It was a strange place. The walls were faced with stone. They were smooth and almost polished-looking. Driven into them at intervals were iron candelabra, some of which had the remains of wax candles in them. Elena could not see the other end of the room, but the flashlight showed a wrought-iron gate quite close, like the gate in some churches used to screen off an altar.

Bonnie was just reaching the bottom of the rung ladder. She waited silently while the others descended, first Matt, then Meredith, then Alaric with the other flashlight.

Elena looked up. "Damon?"

She could see his silhouette against the lighter black rectangle that was the tomb's opening to the sky. "Well?"

"Are you with us?" she asked. Not "Are you *coming* with us?" She knew he would understand the difference.

She waited five heartbeats in the silence that followed. Six, seven, eight . . .

There was a rush of air, and Damon landed neatly. But he didn't look at Elena. His eyes were oddly distant, and she could read nothing in his face.

"It's a crypt," Alaric was saying in wonder, as his flashlight scythed through the darkness. "An underground chamber beneath a church, used as a burial place. They're usually built under larger churches."

Bonnie walked straight up to the scrolled gate and placed one small white hand on it, opening it. It swung away from her.

Elena's heartbeats were coming too quickly to count now. Somehow she forced her legs to move forward, to follow Bonnie. Her sharpened senses were almost painfully acute, but they could tell her nothing about what she was walking into. The beam from Stefan's flashlight was so narrow, and it showed only the rock floor ahead, and Bonnie's enigmatic form.

Bonnie stopped.

This is it, thought Elena, her breath catching in her throat. Oh, my God, this is it; this is really it. She had the sudden intense sensation of being in the middle of a lucid dream, one where she knew she was dreaming but couldn't change anything or wake up. Her muscles deadlocked.

She could smell fear from the others, and she could feel the sharp edge of it from Stefan beside her. His flashlight skimmed over objects beyond Bonnie, but at first Elena's eyes could make no sense of them. She saw angles, planes, contours, and then something leaped into focus. A dead-white face, hanging grotesquely sideways . . .

The scream never got out of her throat. It was only a statue, and the features were familiar. They were the same as on the lid of the tomb above. This tomb was the twin of the one they had come through. Except that this one had been ravaged, the stone lid broken in two and flung against the wall of the crypt. Something was scattered about the floor like fragile ivory sticks. Bits of marble, Elena told her brain desperately; it's only marble, bits of marble.

They were human bones, splintered and crushed.

Bonnie turned around.

Her heart-shaped face swung as if those fixed blank eyes were surveying the group. She ended directly facing Elena.

Then, with a shudder, she stumbled and pitched violently forward like a marionette whose strings have been cut.

Elena barely caught her, half falling herself. "Bonnie? Bonnie?" The brown eyes that looked up at her, dilated and disoriented, were Bonnie's own frightened eyes. "But what happened?" Elena demanded. "Where did it go?"

"I am here."

Above the plundered tomb, a hazy light was showing. No, not a light, Elena thought. She was sensing it with her eyes, but it was not light in the normal spectrum. This was something stranger than infrared or ultraviolet, something human senses had not been built to see. It was being revealed to her, forced on her brain, by some outside Power.

"The Other Power," she whispered, her blood freezing.

"No, Elena."

The voice was not sound, in the same way that the vision was not light. It was quiet as star shine, and sad. It reminded her of something.

Mother? she thought wildly. But it wasn't her mother's voice. The glow above the tomb seemed to swirl and eddy, and for a moment Elena glimpsed in it a face, a gentle, sad face. And then she knew.

"I've been waiting for you," Honoria Fell's voice said softly. "Here I can speak to you at last in my own form, and not through Bonnie's lips. Listen to me. Your time is short, and the danger is very great."

Elena found her tongue. "But what is this room? Why did you bring us here?"

"You asked me to. I couldn't show you until you asked. This is your battleground."

"I don't understand."

"This crypt was built for me by the people of Fell's Church. A resting place for my body. A secret place for one who had secret powers in life. Like Bonnie, I knew things no one else could know. I saw things no one else could see."

"You were psychic," Bonnie whispered huskily.

"In those days, they called it witchery. But I never used my powers for harm, and when I died they built me this monument so that my husband and I could lie in peace. But then, after many years, our peace was disturbed."

The eldritch light ebbed and flowed, Honoria's form wavering. "Another Power came to Fell's Church, full of hatred and destruction. It defiled my resting place and scattered my bones. It made its home here. It went out to work evil against my town. I woke.

"I have tried to warn you against it from the beginning, Elena. It lives here below the graveyard. It has been waiting for you, watching you. Sometimes in the form of an owl—"

An owl. Elena's mind raced ahead. An owl,

like the owl she had seen nesting in the belfry of the church. Like the owl that had been in the barn, like the owl in the black locust tree by her house.

White owl . . . hunting bird . . . flesh eater . . . she thought. And then she remembered great white wings that seemed to stretch to the horizon on either side. A great bird made of mist or snow, coming after her, focused on her, full of bloodlust and animal hate . . .

"No!" she cried, memory engulfing her.

She felt Stefan's hands on her shoulders, his fingers digging in almost painfully. It brought her back to reality. Honoria Fell was still speaking.

"And you, Stefan, it has been watching you. It hated you before it hated Elena. It has been tormenting you and playing with you like a cat with a mouse. It hates those you love. It is full of poisoned love itself."

Elena looked involuntarily behind her. She saw Meredith, Alaric, and Matt standing frozen. Bonnie and Stefan were next to her. But Damon . . . where was Damon?

"Its hatred has grown so great that any death will do, any blood spilled will give it pleasure. Right now, the animals it controls are slinking out of the woods. They are moving toward the town, toward the lights."

"The Snow Dance!" Meredith said sharply.

"Yes. And this time they will kill until the last of them is killed."

"We have to warn those people," Matt said. "Everyone at that dance—"

"You will never be safe until the mind that controls them is destroyed. The killing will go on. You must destroy the Power that hates; that is why I have brought you here."

There was another flux in the light; it seemed to be receding. "You have the courage, if you can find it. Be strong. This is the only help I can give you."

"Wait—please—" Elena began.

The voice continued relentlessly, taking no heed of her. "Bonnie, you have a choice. Your secret powers are a responsibility. They are also a gift, and one that can be taken away. Do you choose to relinquish them?"

"I—" Bonnie shook her head, frightened. "I don't know. I need time. . . ."

"There is no time. Choose." The light was dwindling, caving in on itself.

Bonnie's eyes were bewildered and uncertain as she searched Elena's face for help. "It's *your* choice," Elena whispered. "You have to decide for yourself."

Slowly, the uncertainty left Bonnie's face, and she nodded. She stood away from Elena, without support, turning back to the light. "I'll keep them," she said huskily. "I'll deal with them somehow. My grandmother did."

There was a flicker of something like amusement from the light. "You've chosen wisely. May you use them as well. This is the last time I will speak to you."

"But—"

"I have earned my rest. The fight is yours." And the glow faded, like the last embers of a dying fire.

With it gone, Elena could feel the pressure all around her. Something was going to happen. Some crushing force was coming toward them, or hanging over them. "Stefan—"

Stefan felt it too; she could tell. "Come on," Bonnie said, her voice panicked. "We have to get out of here."

"We have to get to the dance," Matt gasped. His face was white. "We have to help them—"

"Fire," cried Bonnie, looking startled, as if the thought had just come to her. "Fire won't kill them, but it will hold them off—"

"Didn't you listen? We have to face the Other Power. And it's *here*, right here, right now. We can't go!" Elena cried. Her mind was filled with turmoil. Images, memories, and a dreadful foreboding. Bloodlust . . . she could feel it. . . .

"Alaric." Stefan spoke with the ring of command. "You go back. Take the others; do what you can. I'll stay—"

"I think we all should leave!" Alaric shouted. He had to shout to be heard over the deafening noise surrounding them.

His weaving flashlight showed Elena something she hadn't noticed before. In the wall next to her was a gaping hole, as if the stone facing had been ripped away. And beyond was a tunnel into the raw earth, black and endless.

Where does it go? Elena wondered, but the thought was lost among the tumult of her fear. White owl . . . hunting bird . . . flesh eater . . . *crow*, she thought, and suddenly she knew with blinding clarity what she was afraid of.

"Where's Damon?" she screamed, dragging Stefan around as she turned, looking. "Where's Damon?"

"Get *out!*" cried Bonnie, her voice shrill

with terror. She threw herself toward the gate just as the sound split the darkness.

It was a snarl, but not a dog's snarl. It could never be mistaken for that. It was so much deeper, heavier, more resonant. It was a *huge* sound, and it reeked of the jungle, of the hunting bloodlust. It reverberated in Elena's chest, jarred her bones.

It paralyzed her.

The sound came again, hungry and savage, but somehow almost lazy. That confident. And with it came heavy footfalls from the tunnel.

Bonnie was trying to scream, making only a thin whistling sound. In the blackness of the tunnel, something was coming. A shape that moved with a rangy feline swing. Elena recognized the snarl now. It was the sound of the largest of the hunting cats, larger than a lion. The tiger's eyes showed yellow as it reached the end of the tunnel.

And then everything happened at once.

Elena felt Stefan try to pull her backward to get her out of the way. But her own petrified muscles were a hindrance to him, and she knew that it was too late.

The tiger's leap was grace itself, powerful muscles launching it into the air. In that instant, she saw it as if caught in the light of a flashbulb, and her mind noted the lean shining flanks and the supple backbone. But her voice screamed out on its own.

"Damon, no!"

It was only as the black wolf sprang out of the darkness to meet it that she realized the tiger was white.

The great cat's rush was thrown off by the wolf, and Elena felt Stefan wrench her out of the way, pulling her sideways to safety. Her muscles had melted like snowflakes, and she yielded numbly as he put her against the wall. The lid of the tomb was between her and the snarling white shape now, but the gate was on the other side of the fight.

Elena's own weakness was part terror and part bewilderment. She didn't understand anything; confusion roared in her ears. A moment ago she had been certain Damon had been playing with them all this time, that he had been the Other Power all along. But the malice and the bloodlust that emanated from the tiger were unmistakable. This was what had chased her in the graveyard, and from the boardinghouse to the river and her death. This white Power that the wolf was fighting to kill.

It was an impossible match. The black wolf, vicious and aggressive though it might be, didn't stand a chance. One swipe of the tiger's huge claws laid the wolf's shoulder open to the bone. Its jaws snarled open as it tried to get a bone-cracking grip on the wolf's neck.

But then Stefan was there, training the blaze of the flashlight into the cat's eyes, thrusting the wounded wolf out of the way. Elena wished she could scream, wished she could do something to release this rushing ache inside her. She didn't understand; she didn't understand anything. Stefan was in danger. But she couldn't move.

"Get out!" Stefan was shouting to the others. "Do it now; get out!"

Faster than any human, he darted out of the way of a white paw, keeping the light in the tiger's eyes. Meredith was on the other side of the gate now. Matt was half carrying and half dragging Bonnie. Alaric was through.

The tiger lunged and the gate crashed shut. Stefan fell to the side, slipping as he tried to scramble up again.

"We won't leave you—" Alaric cried.

"Go!" shouted Stefan. "Get to the dance; do what you can! *Go!*"

The wolf was attacking again, despite the bleeding wounds in its head, and its shoulder where muscle and tendon lay exposed and shining. The tiger fought back. The animal sounds rose to a volume that Elena couldn't stand. Meredith and the others were gone; Alaric's flashlight had disappeared.

"Stefan!" she screamed, seeing him poised to jump into the fight again.

If he died, she would die, too. And if she had to die, she wanted it to be with him.

The paralysis left her, and she stumbled toward him, sobbing, reaching out to clutch him tightly. She felt his arm around her as he held her with his body between her and the noise and violence. But she was stubborn, as stubborn as he was. She twisted, and then they faced it together.

The wolf was down. It was lying on its back, and although its fur was too dark to show the blood, a red pool gathered beneath it. The white cat stood above it, jaws gaping inches from the vulnerable black throat.

But the death-dealing bite to the neck didn't come. Instead the tiger raised its head to look at Stefan and Elena.

With a strange calmness, Elena found herself noticing tiny details of its appearance.

The whiskers were straight and slender, like silver wires. Its fur was pure white, striped with faint marks like unburnished gold. White and gold, she thought, remembering the owl in the barn. And that stirred another memory . . . of something she'd seen . . . or something she'd heard about. . . .

With a heavy swipe, the cat sent the flashlight flying out of Stefan's hand. Elena heard him hiss in pain, but she could no longer see anything in the blackness. Where there was no light at all, even a hunter was blind. Clinging to him, she waited for the pain of the killing blow.

But suddenly her head was reeling; it was full of gray and spinning fog and she couldn't hold on to Stefan. She couldn't think; she couldn't speak. The floor seemed to be dropping away from her. Dimly, she realized that Power was being used against her, that it was overwhelming her mind.

She felt Stefan's body giving, slumping, falling away from her, and she could no longer resist the fog. She fell forever and never knew when she hit the ground.

Fourteen

White owl . . . hunting bird . . . hunter
. . . tiger. Playing with you like a cat with a
mouse. Like a cat . . . a great cat . . . a kitten. A white kitten.

Death is in the house.

And the kitten, the kitten had run from
Damon. Not out of fear, but out of the fear of
being discovered. Like when it had stood on
Margaret's chest and wailed at the sight of
Elena outside the window.

Elena moaned and almost surfaced from
unconsciousness, but the gray fog dragged her
back under before she could open her eyes.
Her thoughts seethed around her again.

Poisoned love . . . Stefan, it hated you
before it hated Elena. . . . White and gold

. . . *something white . . . something white under the tree . . .*

This time, when she struggled to open her eyes, she succeeded. And even before she could focus in the dim and shifting light, she knew. She finally knew.

The figure in the trailing white dress turned from the candle she was lighting, and Elena saw what might have been her own face on its shoulders. But it was a subtly distorted face, pale and beautiful as an ice sculpture, but *wrong*. It was like the endless reflections of herself Elena had seen in her dream of the hall of mirrors. Twisted and hungry, and mocking.

"Hello, Katherine," she whispered.

Katherine smiled, a sly and predatory smile. "You're not as stupid as I thought," she said.

Her voice was light and sweet—silvery, Elena thought. Like her eyelashes. There were silvery lights in her dress when she moved, too. But her hair was gold, almost as pale a gold as Elena's own. Her eyes were like the kitten's eyes: round and jewel blue. At her throat she wore a necklace with a stone of the same vivid color.

Elena's own throat was sore, as if she had been screaming. It felt dry as well. When she turned her head slowly to the side, even that little motion hurt.

Stefan was beside her, slumped forward, bound by his arms to the wrought-iron pickets of the gate. His head sagged against his chest, but what she could see of his face was deathly white. His throat was torn, and blood had dripped onto his collar and dried.

Elena turned back to Katherine so quickly that her head spun. "Why? Why did you do that?"

Katherine smiled, showing pointed white teeth. "Because I *love* him," she said in a childish singsong. "Don't you love him, too?"

It was only then that Elena fully realized why she couldn't move, and why her arms hurt. She was tied up like Stefan, lashed securely to the closed gate. A painful turning of her head to the other side revealed Damon.

He was in worse shape than his brother. His jacket and arm were ripped open, and the sight of the wound made Elena sick. His shirt hung in tatters, and Elena could see the tiny movement of his ribs as he breathed. If it hadn't been for that, she would have thought he was dead. Blood matted his hair and ran into his closed eyes.

"Which one do you like better?" Katherine

241

asked, in an intimate, confiding tone. "You can tell me. Which one do you think is best?"

Elena looked at her, sickened. "Katherine," she whispered. "Please. Please listen to me. . . ."

"Tell me. Go on." Those jewel blue eyes filled Elena's vision as Katherine leaned in close, her lips almost touching Elena's. "*I* think they're both fun. Do you like fun, Elena?"

Revolted, Elena shut her eyes and turned her face away. If only her head would stop spinning.

Katherine stepped back with a clear laugh. "I know, it's so hard to choose." She did a little pirouette, and Elena saw that what she had vaguely taken for the train to Katherine's dress was Katherine's hair. It flowed like molten gold down her back to spill over the floor, trailing behind her.

"It all depends on your taste," Katherine continued, doing a few graceful dance steps and ending up in front of Damon. She looked over at Elena impishly. "But then I have such a sweet tooth." She grasped Damon by the hair, and, yanking his head up, sank her teeth into his neck.

"No! Don't do that; don't hurt him any

more. . . ." Elena tried to surge forward, but she was tied too tightly. The gate was solid iron, set in stone, and the ropes were sturdy. Katherine was making animal sounds, gnawing and chewing at the flesh, and Damon moaned even in unconsciousness. Elena saw his body jerk reflexively with pain.

"Please stop; oh, please stop—"

Katherine lifted her head. Blood was running down her chin. "But I'm hungry and he's so *good*," she said. She reared back and struck again, and Damon's body spasmed. Elena cried out.

I was like that, she thought. In the beginning, that first night in the woods, I was like that. I hurt Stefan like that, I wanted to kill him. . . .

Darkness swept up around her, and she gave in to it gratefully.

Alaric's car skewed on a patch of ice as it reached the school, and Meredith almost ran into it. She and Matt jumped out of her car, leaving the doors open. Ahead, Alaric and Bonnie did the same.

"What about the rest of the town?" Meredith shouted, running toward them. The wind was rising, and her face burned with frost.

"Just Elena's family—Aunt Judith and Margaret," Bonnie cried. Her voice was shrill and frightened, but there was a look of concentration in her eyes. She leaned her head back as if trying to remember something, and said, "Yes, that's it. They're the other ones the dogs will be after. Make them go somewhere —like the cellar. Keep them there!"

"I'll do it. You three take the dance!"

Bonnie turned to run after Alaric. Meredith raced back to her car.

The dance was in the last stages of breaking up. As many couples were outside as inside, starting toward the parking lot. Alaric shouted at them as he and Matt and Bonnie came pounding up.

"Go back in! Get everybody inside and shut the doors!" he yelled at the sheriff's officers.

But there wasn't time. He reached the cafeteria just as the first lurking shape in the darkness did. One officer went down without a sound or a chance to fire his gun.

Another was quicker, and a gunshot rang out, amplified by the concrete courtyard. Students screamed and began to run away from it, into the parking lot. Alaric went after them, yelling, trying to herd them back.

Other shapes came out of the darkness, from between parked cars, from all sides. Panic ensued. Alaric kept shouting, kept trying to gather the terrified students toward the building. Out here they were easy prey.

In the courtyard, Bonnie turned to Matt. "We need fire!" she said. Matt darted into the cafeteria and came out with a box half-full of dance programs. He threw it to the ground, groping in his pockets for one of the matches they'd used to light the candle before.

The paper caught and burned brightly. It formed an island of safety. Matt continued to wave people into the cafeteria doors behind it. Bonnie plunged inside, to find a scene just as riotous as outside.

She looked around for someone in authority but couldn't see any adults, only panicked kids. Then the red and green crepe paper decorations caught her eye.

The noise was thunderous; even a shout couldn't be heard in here. Struggling past the people trying to get out, she made it to the far side of the room. Caroline was there, looking pale without her summer tan, and wearing the snow queen tiara. Bonnie towed her to the microphone.

"You're good at talking. Tell them to get inside and *stay* in! Tell them to start taking down the decorations. We need anything that'll burn—wood chairs, stuff in garbage cans, *anything.* Tell them it's our only chance!" She added, as Caroline stared at her, frightened and uncomprehending: "You've got the crown on now—so *do* something with it!"

She didn't wait to see Caroline obey. She plunged again into the furor of the room. A moment later she heard Caroline's voice, first hesitant and then urgent, on the loudspeakers.

It was dead quiet when Elena opened her eyes again.

"Elena?"

At the hoarse whisper, she tried to focus and found herself looking into pain-filled green eyes.

"Stefan," she said. She leaned toward him yearningly, wishing she could move. It didn't make sense, but she felt that if they could only hold each other it wouldn't be so bad.

There was a childish laugh. Elena didn't

turn toward it, but Stefan did. Elena saw his reaction, saw the sequence of expressions passing across his face almost too quickly to identify. Blank shock, disbelief, dawning joy —and then horror. A horror that finally turned his eyes blind and opaque.

"Katherine," he said. "But that's impossible. It can't be. You're dead. . . ."

"Stefan . . ." Elena said, but he didn't respond.

Katherine put a hand in front of her mouth and giggled behind it.

"You wake up, too," she said, looking on the other side of Elena. Elena felt a surge of Power. After a moment Damon's head lifted slowly, and he blinked.

There was no astonishment in his face. He leaned his head back, eyes wearily narrowed, and looked for a minute or so at his captor. Then he smiled, a faint and painful smile, but recognizable.

"Our sweet little white kitten," he whispered. "I should have known."

"You didn't know, though, did you?" Katherine said, as eager as a child playing a game. "Even you didn't guess. I fooled everyone." She laughed again. "It was so much fun, watching you while you were watching Stefan, and neither of you knew I was there. I even scratched you once!" Hooking her fingers into claws, she mimicked a kitten's slash.

"At Elena's house. Yes, I remember," Damon said slowly. He didn't seem so much angry as vaguely, whimsically amused. "Well, you're certainly a hunter. The lady *and* the tiger, as it were."

"And I put Stefan in that well," Katherine bragged. "I saw you two fighting; I liked that. I followed Stefan to the edge of the woods, and then—" She clapped her cupped hands together, like someone catching a moth. Opening them slowly, she peered down into them as if she really had something there, and giggled secretly. "I was going to keep him to play with," she confided. Then her lower lip thrust out and she looked at Elena balefully. "But you took him. That was mean, Elena. You shouldn't have done that."

The dreadful childish slyness was gone from her face, and for a moment Elena glimpsed the searing hatred of a woman.

"Greedy girls get punished," Katherine said, moving toward her, "and you're a greedy girl."

"Katherine!" Stefan had woken from his

daze, and he spoke quickly. "Don't you want to tell us what else you've done?"

Distracted, Katherine stepped back. She looked surprised, then flattered.

"Well—if you really want me to," she said. She hugged her elbows with her hands and pirouetted again, her golden hair twisting on the floor. "No," she said gleefully, turning back and pointing at them. "You guess. You guess and I'll tell you 'right' or 'wrong.' Go on!"

Elena swallowed, casting a covert glance at Stefan. She didn't see the point of stalling Katherine; it was all going to come out the same in the end. But some instinct told her to hang on to life as long as she could.

"You attacked Vickie," she said, carefully. Her own voice sounded winded to her ears, but she was positive now. "The girl in the ruined church that night."

"Good! Yes," Katherine cried. She made another kitten swipe with clawed fingers. "Well, after all, she was in my church," she added reasonably. "And what she and that boy were doing—well! You don't do that in church. So, I *scratched* her!" Katherine drew out the word, demonstrating, like somebody telling a story to a young child. "And . . . I licked the blood up!" She licked pale pink lips with her tongue. Then she pointed at Stefan. "Next guess!"

"You've been hounding her ever since," Stefan said. He wasn't playing the game; he was making a sickened observation.

"Yes, we're done with that! Go on to something else," Katherine said sharply. But then she fiddled with the buttons at the neck of her dress, her fingers twinkling. And Elena thought of Vickie, with her startled-fawn eyes, undressing in the cafeteria in front of everyone. "I made her do silly things." Katherine laughed. "She was fun to play with."

Elena's arms were numb and cramped. She realized that she was reflexively straining against the ropes, so offended by Katherine's words that she couldn't hold still. She made herself stop, trying instead to lean back and get a little feeling into her deadened hands. What she was going to do if she got free she didn't know, but she had to try.

"Next *guess*," Katherine was saying dangerously.

"Why do you say it's your church?" Damon asked. His voice was still distantly amused, as if none of this affected him at all. "What about Honoria Fell?"

"Oh, that old spook!" Katherine said maliciously. She peered around behind Elena, her mouth pursed, her eyes glaring. Elena realized for the first time that they were facing the entrance to the crypt, with the ransacked tomb behind them. Maybe Honoria would help them. . . .

But then she remembered that quiet, fading voice. *This is the only help I can give you.* And she knew that no further aid would come.

As if she'd read Elena's thoughts, Katherine was saying, "She can't do *anything*. She's just a pack of old bones." The graceful hands made gestures as if Katherine were breaking those bones. "All she can do is talk, and lots of times I stopped you from hearing her." Katherine's expression was dark again, and Elena felt an acid twinge of fear.

"You killed Bonnie's dog, Yangtze," she said. It was a random guess, thrown out to divert Katherine, but it worked.

"Yes! That was funny. You all came running out of the house and started moaning and crying. . . ." Katherine evoked the scene in pantomime: the little dog lying in front of Bonnie's house, the girls rushing out to find his body. "He tasted bad, but it was worth it. I followed Damon there when he was a crow. I used to follow him a lot. If I wanted I could have grabbed that crow, and . . ." She made a sharp wringing motion.

Bonnie's dream, thought Elena, icy revelation sweeping over her. She didn't even realize she'd spoken aloud until she saw Stefan and Katherine looking at her. "Bonnie dreamed about you," she whispered. "But she thought it was me. She told me that she saw me standing under a tree with the wind blowing. And she was afraid of me. She said I looked different, pale but almost glowing. And a crow flew by and I grabbed it and wrung its neck." Bile was rising in Elena's throat, and she gulped it down. "But it was you," she said.

Katherine looked delighted, as if Elena had somehow proved her point. "People dream about me a lot," she said smugly. "Your aunt —she's dreamed about me. I tell her it was her fault you died. She thinks it's you telling her."

"Oh, God . . ."

"I wish you *had* died," Katherine went on, her face turning spiteful. "You *should* have died. I kept you in the river long enough. But you were such a tramp, getting blood from both of them, that you came back. Oh, well." She gave a furtive smile. "Now I can play with you longer. I lost my temper that day, because I saw Stefan had given you my ring. My ring!" Her voice rose. "Mine, that I left for them to remember me by. And he gave it to *you*. That was when I knew I wasn't just going to play with him. I had to kill him."

Stefan's eyes were stricken, confounded. "But I thought you were dead," he said. "You *were* dead, five hundred years ago. Katherine . . ."

"Oh, that was the first time I fooled you," Katherine said, but there was no glee in her tone now. It was sullen. "I arranged it all with Gudren, my maid. The two of you wouldn't accept my choice," she burst out, looking from Stefan to Damon angrily. "I wanted us all to be happy; I loved you. I loved you both. But that wasn't good enough for you."

Katherine's face had changed again, and Elena saw in it the hurt child of five centuries ago. That must have been what Katherine looked like, *then*, she thought wonderingly. The wide blue eyes were actually filling with tears.

"I wanted you to love each other,"

Katherine went on, sounding bewildered, "but you wouldn't. And I felt awful. I thought if you thought I'd died, that you *would* love each other. And I knew I had to go away, anyway, before Papa started to suspect what I was.

"So Gudren and I arranged it," she said softly, lost in memory. "I had another talisman against the sun made, and I gave her my ring. And she took my white dress—my best white dress—and ashes from the fireplace. We burned fat there so the ashes would smell right. And she put them out in the sun, where you would find them, along with my note. I wasn't sure you'd be fooled, but you were.

"But then"—Katherine's face twisted in grief—"you did everything all *wrong*. You were supposed to be sorry, and cry, and comfort each other. I did it for *you*. But instead you ran and got swords. Why did you *do* that?" It was a cry from the heart. "Why didn't you *take* my gift? You treated it like garbage. I told you in the note that I wanted you to be reconciled with each other. But you didn't listen and you got swords. You killed each other. *Why* did you do it?"

Tears were slipping down Katherine's

cheeks, and Stefan's face was wet, too. "We were stupid," he said, as caught up in the memory of the past as she was. "We blamed each other for your death, and we were so stupid. . . . Katherine, listen to me. It was my fault; I was the one who attacked first. And I've been sorry—you don't know how sorry I've been ever since. You don't know how many times I've thought about it and wished there was something I could do to change it. I'd have given anything to take it back—*anything*. I killed my brother. . . ." His voice cracked, and tears spilled from his eyes. Elena, her heart breaking with grief, turned helplessly to Damon and saw that he wasn't even aware of her. The look of amusement was gone, and his eyes were fixed on Stefan in utter concentration, riveted.

"Katherine, please listen to me," Stefan said shakily, regaining his voice. "We've all hurt one another enough. Please let us go now. Or keep me, if you want, but let them leave. I'm the one that's to blame. Keep me, and I'll do whatever you want. . . ."

Katherine's jewel-like eyes were liquid and impossibly blue, filled with an endless sorrow. Elena didn't dare to breathe, afraid to break the spell as the slender girl moved toward Stefan, her face softened and yearning.

But then the ice inside Katherine crept out again, freezing the tears on her cheeks. "You should have thought of that a long time ago," she said. "I might have listened to you then. I was sorry you'd killed each other at first. I ran away, without even Gudren, back to my home. But then I didn't have *anything*, not even a new dress, and I was hungry and cold. I might have starved if Klaus hadn't found me."

Klaus. Through her dismay, Elena remembered something Stefan had told her. Klaus was the man who'd made Katherine a vampire, the man the villagers said was evil.

"*Klaus* taught me the truth," Katherine said. "He showed me how the world really is. You have to be strong, and take the things you want. You have to think only of yourself. And I'm the strongest of all now. I am. You know how I got that way?" She answered the question without even waiting for them to respond. "Lives. So many lives. Humans and vampires, and they're all inside *me* now. I killed Klaus after a century or two. He was *surprised*. He didn't know how much I'd learned.

"I was so happy, taking lives, filling myself up with them. But then I would remember *you*, you two, and what you did. How you treated my gift. And I knew I had to punish you. I finally figured out how to do it.

"I brought you here, both of you. I put the thought in your mind, Stefan, the way you put thoughts into a human's. I guided you to this place. And then I made sure Damon followed you. Elena was here. I think she must be related to me somehow; she looks like me. I knew you'd see her and feel guilty. But you weren't supposed to fall in love with her!" The resentfulness in Katherine's voice gave way to fury again. "You weren't supposed to forget me! You weren't supposed to give her my ring!"

"Katherine . . ."

Katherine swept on. "Oh, you made me so angry. And now I'm going to make you sorry, really sorry. I know who I hate most now, and it's you, Stefan. Because I loved you best." She seemed to regain control of herself, wiping the last traces of tears from her face and drawing herself up with exaggerated dignity.

"I don't hate Damon as much," she said. "I might even let him live." Her eyes narrowed, and then widened with an idea. "Listen, Damon," she said secretly. "You're not as stupid as Stefan is. You know the way things really are. I've heard you say it. I've seen things you've done." She leaned forward. "I've been lonely since Klaus died. You could keep me company. All you have to do is say you love me best. Then after I kill them we'll go away. You can even kill the girl if you want. I'd let you. What do you think?"

Oh, God, thought Elena, sickened again. Damon's eyes were on Katherine's wide blue ones; he seemed to be searching her face. And the whimsical amusement was back in his expression. Oh, God, no, Elena thought. Please, no . . .

Slowly, Damon smiled.

Fifteen

Elena watched Damon with mute dread. She knew that disturbing smile too well. But even as her heart sank, her mind threw a mocking question at her. What difference did it make? She and Stefan were going to die anyway. It only made sense for Damon to save himself. And it was wrong to expect him to go against his nature.

She watched that beautiful, capricious smile with a feeling of sorrow for what Damon might have been.

Katherine smiled back at him, enchanted. "We'll be so happy together. Once they're dead, I'll let you go. I didn't mean to hurt you, not really. I just got angry." She put out a slender hand and stroked his cheek. "I'm sorry."

"Katherine," he said. He was still smiling.

"Yes." She leaned closer.

"Katherine . . ."

"Yes, Damon?"

"Go to hell."

Elena flinched from what happened next before it happened, feeling the violent upsurge of Power, of malevolent, unbridled Power. She screamed at the change in Katherine. That lovely face was twisting, mutating into something that was neither human nor animal. A red light blazed in Katherine's eyes as she fell on Damon, her fangs sinking into his throat.

Talons sprang from her fingertips, and she raked Damon's already-bleeding chest with it, tearing into his skin while the blood flowed. Elena kept screaming, realizing dimly that the pain in her arms was from fighting the ropes that held her. She heard Stefan shouting, too, but above everything she heard the deafening shriek of Katherine's mental voice.

Now you'll be sorry! Now I'm going to make you sorry! I'll kill you! I'll kill you! I'll kill you! I'll kill you!

The words themselves hurt, like daggers

stabbing into Elena's mind. The sheer Power of it stupefied her, rocking her back against the iron pickets. But there was no way to get away from it. It seemed to echo from all around her, hammering in her skull.

Kill you! Kill you! Kill you!

Elena fainted.

Meredith, crouched beside Aunt Judith in the utility room, shifted her weight, straining to interpret the sounds outside the door. The dogs had gotten into the cellar; she wasn't sure how, but from the bloody muzzles of some of them, she thought they had broken through the ground-level windows. Now they were outside the utility room, but Meredith couldn't tell what they were doing. It was too quiet out there.

Margaret, huddled on Robert's lap, whimpered once.

"Hush," Robert whispered quickly. "It's all right, sweetheart. Everything's going to be all right."

Meredith met his frightened, determined eyes over Margaret's tow head. We almost had you pegged for the Other Power, she thought. But there was no time to regret it now.

"Where's Elena? Elena said she'd watch

over me," Margaret said, her eyes large and solemn. "She said she'd take care of me." Aunt Judith put a hand to her mouth.

"She is taking care of you," Meredith whispered. "She just sent me to do it, that's all. It's the *truth*," she added fiercely, and saw Robert's look of reproach melt into perplexity.

Outside, the silence had given way to scratching and gnawing sounds. The dogs were at work on the door.

Robert cradled Margaret's head closer to his chest.

Bonnie didn't know how long they had been working. Hours, certainly. Forever, it seemed like. The dogs had gotten in through the kitchen and the old wooden side doors. So far, though, only about a dozen had gotten past the fires lit like barricades in front of these openings. And the men with guns had taken care of most of those.

But Mr. Smallwood and his friends were now holding empty rifles. And they were running out of things to burn.

Vickie had gotten hysterical a little while ago, screaming and holding her head as if something was hurting her. They'd been looking for ways to restrain her when she finally passed out.

Bonnie went up to Matt, who was looking out over the fire through the demolished side door. He wasn't looking for dogs, she knew, but for something else much farther away. Something you couldn't see from here.

"You had to go, Matt," she said. "There was nothing else you could do." He didn't answer or turn around.

"It's almost dawn," she said. "Maybe when that comes, the dogs will leave." But even as she said it, she knew it wasn't true.

Matt didn't answer. She touched his shoulder. "Stefan's with her. Stefan's there."

At last, Matt gave some response. He nodded. "Stefan's there," he said.

Brown and snarling, another shape charged out of the dark.

It was much later when Elena came gradually to consciousness. She knew because she could see, not just by the handful of candles Katherine had lit but also by the cold gray dimness that filtered down from the crypt's opening.

She could see Damon, too. He was lying on the floor, his bonds slashed along with his clothes. There was enough light now to see the full extent of his wounds, and Elena wondered if he was still alive. He was motionless enough to be dead.

Damon? she thought. It was only after she had done it that she realized the word had not been spoken. Somehow, Katherine's shrieking had closed a circuit in her mind, or maybe it had awakened something sleeping. And Matt's blood had undoubtedly helped, giving her the strength to finally find her mental voice.

She turned her head the other way. *Stefan?*

His face was haggard with pain, but aware. Too aware. Elena almost wished that he were as insensible as Damon to what was happening to them.

Elena, he returned.

Where is she? Elena said, her eyes moving slowly around the room.

Stefan looked toward the opening of the crypt. *She went up there a while ago. Maybe to check on how the dogs are doing.*

Elena had thought she'd reached the limit of fear and dread, but it wasn't true. She hadn't remembered the others then.

Elena, I'm sorry. Stefan's face was filled with what no words could express.

It's not your fault, Stefan. You didn't do this to her. She did it to herself. Or—it just happened to her, because of what she is. What we are. Running beneath Elena's thoughts was the memory of how she had attacked Stefan in the woods, and how she had felt when she was racing toward Mr. Smallwood, planning her revenge. *It could have been me,* she said.

No! You could never become like that.

Elena didn't answer. If she had the Power now, what would she do to Katherine? What *wouldn't* she do to her? But she knew it would only upset Stefan more to talk about it.

I thought Damon was going to betray us, she said.

I did, too, said Stefan queerly. He was looking at his brother with an odd expression.

Do you still hate him?

Stefan's gaze darkened. *No,* he said quietly. *No, I don't hate him anymore.*

Elena nodded. It was important, somehow. Then she started, her nerves hyper-alert, as something shadowed the entrance to the crypt. Stefan tensed, too.

She's coming. Elena—

I love you, Stefan, Elena said hopelessly, as the misty white shape hurtled down.

Katherine took form in front of them.

"I don't know what's happening," she said, looking annoyed. "You're blocking my tunnel." She peered behind Elena again, toward the broken tomb and the hole in the wall. "That's what I use for getting around," she went on, seemingly unaware of Damon's body at her feet. "It goes beneath the river. So I don't have to cross over running water, you see. Instead, I cross *under* it." She looked at them as if waiting for their appreciation of the joke.

Of course, thought Elena. How could I have been so stupid? Damon rode with us in Alaric's car over the river. He crossed running water then, and probably lots of other times. He couldn't have been the Other Power.

It was strange how she could think even though she was so frightened. It was as if one part of her mind stood watching from a distance.

"I'm going to kill you now," Katherine said conversationally. "Then I'm going under the river to kill your friends. I don't think the dogs have done it yet. But I'll take care of it myself."

"Let Elena go," said Stefan. His voice was quenched but compelling all the same.

"I haven't decided how to do it," said Katherine, ignoring him. "I might roast you. There's almost enough light for that now. And I've got these." She reached down the front of her gown and brought her closed hand out. "One—two—three!" she said, dropping two silver rings and a gold one onto the ground. Their stones shone blue as Katherine's eyes, blue as the stone in the necklace at Katherine's throat.

Elena's hands twisted frantically and she felt the smooth bareness of her ring finger. It was true. She wouldn't have believed how naked she felt without that circlet of metal. It was necessary to her life, to her survival. Without it—

"Without these you'll die," Katherine said, scuffing the rings carelessly with the toe of one foot. "But I don't know if that's *slow* enough." She paced back almost to the far wall of the crypt, her silver dress shimmering in the dim light.

It was then that the idea came to Elena.

She could move her hands. Enough to feel one with the other, enough to know that they weren't numb anymore. The ropes were looser.

But Katherine was strong. Unbelievably

strong. And faster than Elena, too. Even if Elena got free she would have time for only one quick act.

She rotated one wrist, feeling the ropes give.

"There are other ways," Katherine said. "I could cut you and watch you bleed. I like watching."

Gritting her teeth, Elena exerted pressure against the rope. Her hand was bent at an excruciating angle, but she continued to press. She felt the burn of the rope slipping aside.

"Or rats," Katherine was saying pensively. "Rats could be fun. I could tell them when to start and when to stop."

Working the other hand free was much easier. Elena tried to give no sign of what was going on behind her back. She would have liked to call to Stefan with her mind, but she didn't dare. Not if there was any chance Katherine might hear.

Katherine's pacing had taken her right up to Stefan. "I think I'll start with you," she said, pushing her face close to his. "I'm hungry again. And you're so sweet, Stefan. I forgot how sweet you were."

There was a rectangle of gray light on the

floor. Dawn light. It was coming in through the crypt's opening. Katherine had already been out in that light. But . . .

Katherine smiled suddenly, her blue eyes sparkling. "I know! I'll drink you almost up and make you watch while I kill *her*! I'll leave you just enough strength so you see her die before you do. Doesn't that sound like a good plan?" Blithely, she clapped her hands and pirouetted again, dancing away.

Just one more step, thought Elena. She saw Katherine approach the rectangle of light. Just one more step . . .

Katherine took the step. "That's it, then!" She started to turn around. "What a good—"

Now!

Yanking her cramped arms out of the last loops of rope, Elena rushed her. It was like the rush of a hunting cat. One desperate sprint to reach the prey. One chance. One hope.

She struck Katherine with her full weight. The impact knocked them both into the rectangle of light. She felt Katherine's head crack against the stone floor.

And felt the searing pain, as if her own body had been plunged into poison. It was a feeling like the burning dryness of hunger, only stronger. A thousand times stronger. It was unbearable.

"Elena!" Stefan screamed, with mind and voice.

Stefan, she thought. Beneath her Power surged as Katherine's stunned eyes focused. Her mouth twisted with rage, fangs bursting forth. They were so long they cut into the lower lip. That distorted mouth opened in a howl.

Elena's clumsy hand fumbled at Katherine's throat. Her fingers closed on the cool metal of Katherine's blue necklace. With all her strength, she wrenched and felt the chain give way. She tried to clasp it, but her fingers felt thick and uncoordinated and Katherine's clawing hand scrabbled at it wildly. It spun away into the shadows.

"Elena!" Stefan called again in that dreadful voice.

She felt as if her body were filled with light. As if she were transparent. Only, light was pain. Beneath her, Katherine's warped face was looking up directly into the winter sky. Instead of a howl, there was a shrieking that went up and up.

Elena tried to lift herself off, but she didn't have the strength. Katherine's face was rifting, cracking open. Lines of fire opened in it. The screaming reached a crescendo. Katherine's hair was aflame, her skin was blackening. Elena felt fire from both above and below.

Then she felt something grab her, seize her shoulders and yank her away. The coolness of the shadows was like ice water. Something was turning her, cradling her.

She saw Stefan's arms, red where they had been exposed to the sun and bleeding where he had torn free of his ropes. She saw his face, saw the stricken horror and grief. Then her eyes blurred and she saw nothing.

Meredith and Robert, striking at the blood-soaked muzzles that thrust through the hole in the door, paused in confusion. The teeth had stopped snapping and tearing. One muzzle jerked and slid out of the way. Edging sideways to look at the other, Meredith saw that the dog's eyes were glazed and milky. They didn't move. She looked at Robert, who stood panting.

There was no more noise from the cellar. Everything was silent.

But they didn't dare to hope.

* * *

Vickie's demented shrieking stopped as if it had been cut with a knife. The dog, which had sunk its teeth into Matt's thigh, stiffened and gave a convulsive shudder; then, its jaws released him. Gasping for breath, Bonnie swung to look beyond the dying fire. There was just enough light to see bodies of other dogs lying where they had fallen outside.

She and Matt leaned on each other, looking around, bewildered.

It had finally stopped snowing.

Slowly, Elena opened her eyes.

Everything was very clear and calm.

She was glad the shrieking was over. That had been bad; it had hurt. Now, nothing hurt. She felt as if her body were filled with light again, but this time there was no pain. It was as if she were floating, very high and easy, on wafts of air. She almost felt she didn't have a body at all.

She smiled.

Turning her head didn't hurt, although it increased the loose, floating feeling. She saw, in the oblong of pale light on the floor, the smoldering remains of a silvery dress. Katherine's lie of five hundred years ago had become the truth.

That was that, then. Elena looked away. She didn't wish anyone harm now, and she didn't want to waste time on Katherine. There were so many more important things.

"Stefan," she said and sighed, and smiled. Oh, this was nice. This must be how a bird felt.

"I didn't mean for things to turn out this way," she said, softly rueful. His green eyes were wet. They filled again, but he returned her smile.

"I know," he said. "I know, Elena."

He understood. That was good; that was important. It was easy to see the things that were really important now. And Stefan's understanding meant more to her than all the world.

It seemed to her that it had been a long while since she'd really looked at him. Since she'd taken time to appreciate how beautiful he was, with his dark hair and his eyes as green as oak leaves. But she saw it now, and she saw his soul shining through those eyes. It was worth it, she thought. I didn't want to die; I don't want to now. But I'd do it all over again if I had to.

"I love you," she whispered.

"I love you," he said, squeezing their joined hands.

The strange, languorous lightness cradled her gently. She could scarcely feel Stefan holding her.

She would have thought she'd be terrified. But she wasn't, not as long as Stefan was there.

"The people at the dance—they'll be all right now, won't they?" she said.

"They'll be all right now," Stefan whispered. "You saved them."

"I didn't get to say good-bye to Bonnie and Meredith. Or Aunt Judith. You have to tell them I love them."

"I'll tell them," Stefan said.

"You can tell them yourself," panted another voice, hoarse and unused sounding. Damon had pulled himself across the floor behind Stefan. His face was ravaged, streaked with blood, but his dark eyes burned at her. "Use your will, Elena. Hold on. You have the strength—"

She smiled at him, waveringly. She knew the truth. What was happening was only finishing what had been started two weeks ago. She'd had thirteen days to get things straight, to make amends with Matt and say good-bye to Margaret. To tell Stefan she loved him. But now the grace period was up.

Still, there was no point in hurting Damon. She loved Damon, too. "I'll try," she promised.

"We'll take you home," he said.

"But not yet," she told him gently. "Let's wait just a little while."

Something happened in the fathomless black eyes, and the burning spark went out. Then she saw that Damon knew, too.

"I'm not afraid," she said. "Well—only a little." A drowsiness had started, and she felt very comfortable, but as if she were falling asleep. Things were drifting away from her.

An ache rose in her chest. She was not much afraid, but she was sorry. There were so many things she would miss, so many things she wished she had done.

"Oh," she said softly. "How funny."

The walls of the crypt seemed to have melted. They were gray and cloudy and there was something like a doorway there, like the door that was the opening to the underground room. Only this was a doorway into a different light.

"How beautiful," she murmured. "Stefan? I'm so tired."

"You can rest now," he whispered.

"You won't let go of me?"

"No."

"Then I won't be afraid."

Something was shining on Damon's face. She reached toward it, touched it, and lifted her fingers away in wonder.

"Don't be sad," she told him, feeling the cool wetness on her fingertips. But a pang of worry disturbed her. Who was there to understand Damon now? Who would be there to push him, to try to see what was really inside him? "You have to take care of each other," she said, realizing it. A little strength came back to her, like a candle flaring in the wind. "Stefan, will you promise? Promise to take care of each other?"

"I promise," he said. "Oh, Elena . . ."

Waves of sleepiness were overcoming her. "That's good," she said. "That's good, Stefan."

The doorway was closer, so close she could touch it now. She wondered if her parents were somewhere behind it.

"Time to go home," she whispered.

And then the darkness and the shadows faded and there was nothing but light.

* * *

Stefan held her while her eyes closed. And then he just held her, the tears he'd been keeping back falling without restraint. It was a different pain than when he'd pulled her out of the river. There was no anger in this, and no hatred, but a love that seemed to go on and on forever.

It hurt even more.

He looked at the rectangle of sunlight, just a step or two away from him. Elena had gone into the light. She'd left him here alone.

Not for long, he thought.

His ring was on the floor. He didn't even glance at it as he rose, his eyes on the shaft of sunlight shining down.

A hand grabbed his arm and pulled him back.

Stefan looked into his brother's face.

Damon's eyes were dark as midnight, and he was holding Stefan's ring. As Stefan watched, unable to move, he forced the ring onto Stefan's finger and released him.

"Now," he said, sinking back painfully, "you can go wherever you want." He picked the ring Stefan had given to Elena off the ground and held it out. "This is yours, too. Take it. Take it and go." He turned his face away.

Stefan gazed at the golden circlet in his palm for a long time.

Then his fingers closed over it and he looked back at Damon. His brother's eyes were shut, his breathing labored. He looked exhausted and in pain.

And Stefan had made a promise to Elena.

"Come on," he said quietly, putting the ring in his pocket. "Let's get you some place where you can rest."

He put an arm around his brother to help him up. And then, for a moment, he just held on.

Sixteen

December 16, Monday

Stefan gave this to me. He's given most of the things in his room away. I said I didn't want it at first, because I didn't know what to do with it. But now I think I have an idea.

People are starting to forget already. They're getting the details wrong, and adding things they just imagined. And, most of all, they're making up explanations. Why it wasn't really supernatural, why there's a rational reason for this or that. It's just silly, but there's no way to stop them, especially the adults.

They're the worst. They're saying the dogs were hydrophobic or something. The vet's come up with a new name for it, some kind of rabies that's spread by bats. Meredith says that's ironic. I think it's just stupid.

The kids are a little better, especially the ones who were at the dance. There are some I think we can rely on, like Sue Carson and Vickie. Vickie's changed so much in the last two days that it's like a miracle. She's not the way she's been for the last two and a half months, but she's not the way she used to be, either. She used to be pretty much of a bimbo, running around with the tough crowd. But now I think she's okay.

Even Caroline wasn't so bad today. She didn't talk at the other service, but she talked at this one. She said Elena was the real snow queen, which was kind of cribbing off of Sue's speech from before, but probably the best Caroline could do. It was a nice gesture.

Elena looked so peaceful. Not like a wax doll, but as if she were sleeping. I know everybody says that, but it's true. This time, it really is true.

But afterward people were talking about "her remarkable escape from drowning" and stuff like that. And saying she died of an embolism or something. Which is absolutely ridiculous. But that's what gave me the idea.

I'm going to get her other diary out of her closet. And then I'm going to ask Mrs. Grimesby to put them in the library, not in a case like Honoria

Fell's, but where people can pick them up and read them. Because the truth is in here. This is where the real story is. And I don't want anybody to forget it.

I think maybe the kids will remember.

I suppose I should put what happened to the rest of the people around here; Elena would want that. Aunt Judith is okay, although she's one of the adults who can't deal with the truth. She needs a rational explanation. She and Robert are going to get married at Christmas. That should be good for Margaret.

Margaret's got the right idea. She told me at the service that she's going to go see Elena and her parents someday, but not now, because there were a lot of things she still had to do right here. I don't know what put that idea into her head. She's smart for a four-year-old.

Alaric and Meredith are also okay, of course. When they saw each other that horrible morning, after everything had quieted down and we were picking up the pieces, they practically fell into each other's arms. I think there's something going on there. Meredith says she'll discuss it when she's eighteen and she graduates.

Typical, absolutely typical. Everybody else gets the guys. I'm thinking of trying one of my grandmother's rituals, just to see if I'll ever get married at all. There isn't even anybody I want to marry around here.

Well, there's Matt. Matt's nice. But right now he's only got one girl on his mind. I don't know if that will ever change.

He punched Tyler in the nose after the service today, because Tyler said something off-color about her. Tyler is one person I know will never change, no matter what. He'll always be the mean, obnoxious jerk he is now.

But Matt—well, Matt's eyes are awfully blue. And he's got a terrific right hook.

Stefan couldn't hit Tyler because he wasn't there. There are still plenty of people in town who think he killed Elena. He must have, they say, because there was nobody else there. Katherine's ashes were scattered all over by the time the rescuers got to the crypt. Stefan says it's because she was so old that she flamed up like that. He says he should have realized the first time, when Katherine pretended to burn, that a young vampire wouldn't turn to ashes that way. She'd just die, like Elena. Only the old ones crumble.

Some people—especially Mr. Smallwood and his friends—would probably blame Damon if they could get hold of him. But they can't. He wasn't there when they reached the tomb, because Stefan helped him get away. Stefan won't say where, but

282

I think to someplace in the woods. Vampires must heal fast because today when I met him after the service, Stefan said that Damon had left Fell's Church. He wasn't happy about it; I think Damon didn't tell him. Now the question seems to be: What is Damon doing? Out biting innocent girls? Or is he reformed? I wouldn't lay bets on it either way. Damon was a strange guy.

But gorgeous. Definitely gorgeous.

Stefan won't say where he's going, either. But I have a sneaking suspicion Damon may get a surprise if he looks behind him. Apparently, Elena made Stefan promise to watch out for him or something. And Stefan takes promises very, very seriously.

I wish him luck. But he'll be doing what Elena wanted him to, which I think will make him happy. As happy as he can be here without her. He's wearing her ring on a chain around his neck now.

If you think any of this sounds frivolous or as if I don't care about Elena, that just shows how wrong you are. I dare anybody to say that to me. Meredith and I cried all day Saturday, and most of Sunday. And I was so angry I wanted to rip things apart and break them. I kept thinking, why Elena? Why? When there were so many other people who could have died that night. Out of the whole town, she was the only one.

Of course, she did it to save them, but why did she have to give her life to do it? It isn't fair.

Oh, I'm starting to cry again. That's what happens when you think about life being fair. And I can't explain why it isn't. I'd like to go bang on Honoria Fell's tomb and ask her if she can explain, but she wouldn't talk to me. I don't think it's something anybody knows.

I loved Elena. And I'm going to miss her terribly. The whole school is. It's like a light that's gone out. Robert says that's what her name means in Latin, "light."

Now there'll always be a part of me where the light has gone away.

I wish I'd been able to say good-bye to her, but Stefan says she sent her love to me. I'm going to try to think of that as a light to take with me.

I'd better stop writing now. Stefan's leaving, and Matt and Meredith and Alaric and I are going to see him off. I didn't mean to get so into this; I've never kept a journal myself. But I want people to know the truth about Elena. She wasn't a saint. She wasn't always sweet and good and honest and agreeable. But she was strong and loving and loyal to her friends, and in the end she did the most unselfish thing anybody could do. Meredith says it means she chose light over darkness. I want people to know that so they'll always remember.

I always will.

—Bonnie McCullough
12/16/91

Here's a preview of the
next terrifying novel by
Nicholas Adams

Santa Claws

One

The snow was still falling lightly from the
dark sky, cutting down visibility somewhat. It
hardly mattered; the wolfling was hunting by
scent, not sight. Still, the foot or so of snow on
the ground, the welcome chill in the air, and
the darkness meant that humans were even less
likely to see it. They'd all be indoors, huddled
next to blazing fires, watching television, eating their pallid, tasteless foods. The wolfling
grinned toothily to itself at these images. Humans! Weak, pitiful, foolish creatures! Not even
fit for real prey . . .

Stopping for a moment, the wolfling sniffed
at the cold air. There, off to the north! That was
the tang it was after! The scent of power, flesh,
teeth, and animal ferocity.

The scent of death.

Heavy muscles moving with practiced ease under its thick fur coat, the wolfling resumed its course. Flurries of snow gathered around it, but the knife-edged wind couldn't penetrate its fur. Loping along, the creature approached the game farm, completely unnoticed by the one or two lonely, homeward-bound drivers foolish enough to be out on a night like this. As the lights of the cars swept slowly past, the wolfling froze, only its yellow, gleaming eyes moving, watching as the cars moved through the darkness. Then it calmly resumed its journey.

There was an eight-foot wooden fence surrounding the game farm. The barbed wire at the top was barely visible in the gloom. The wolfling snorted with contempt. This fence might keep youthful pranksters out, or wandering animals in, but it would hardly be a deterrent to *it*! Pausing, it tensed its strong muscles and sprang into the air. The sharpened barbs of the wire barely grazed the wolfling's stomach fur as the powerful spring took the huge creature easily into the compound on the other side. Even if there had been no snow, the wolfling's landing would have been silent, its large paws absorbing the impact of its weight. Barely breathing harder, it stopped and sniffed the air again.

The scent of its prey was stronger now in its nostrils. Not far to go! Padding along softly, the wolfling began to rely on its uncanny sense of hearing. There would be keepers here, and one might even have decided to brave the winter storm to check on the animals. Best to be ready for anything . . .

There were deer here, of course. Big, swift, stupid creatures. The wolfling could hear them starting to get skittish. It could picture their nervousness, their uncertainty. The deer here had never had to face anything like it before. But they could smell the stench of death surrounding it. Like all victims, they could recognize the strong, the deadly, the hunters. Again, the wolfling curled its lips in a grim smile. The long fangs dripped hot saliva onto the cold snow as it moved through the darkness.

It paused by one compound. An elk! The large beasts were good eating, and they could put on a surprising turn of speed when chased. Stomach rumbling, the wolfling briefly considered going after the elk. Its yellow eyes gleamed in anticipation, the thought of warm blood on its teeth, the exhilaration of the chase. Then, reluctantly, it shook its head. In a place like this, the chase would cause too much noise, and humans might investigate. Their guns could never kill the wolfling, but they hurt. It had a dim memory of one such encounter and didn't want another. It stared at the elk, knowing the animal was quivering with fear in the cloak of the dark. *You're lucky tonight*, the wolfling thought. *Tonight, I let you live. But you may not always be this lucky.* Then, before it could be too strongly tempted, it moved onward.

There, just ahead! The wolfling paused once more, silent in the darkness. There was a slight glow, a flashlight beam impossibly trying to combat the gloom and the falling snow. The dim light burned as the keeper passed along the invisible pathway. As the wolfling had suspected, one of the humans was out, checking on the animals. A woman. The reek of perfume, the telltale body scent that no human could really disguise—at least, not from the wolfling's highly developed sense of smell. The wolfling licked its lips. Perhaps . . . its long front claws flexed, as it imagined the feel of them ripping into human flesh . . .

Stop it! the wolfling told itself, fighting back the desire to kill. Not yet . . . there was still too much to do. Business before pleasure. . . . Unaware of how close she had come to her death, the dim shape of the keeper passed by the waiting wolfling, heading back to the warmth of her office.

Almost whimpering from the fight it had to wage continually with its own nature, the wolfling resumed its way. This had to be done quickly! If it stayed here much longer, the blood-lust would come upon it, and it would do something foolish, something that might alert the nervous, devious humans to its presence.

Then it reached its goal. The too-small cage, the strong odor of meat ripped apart, the smell of the prey. The wolfling's eyes glowed with satisfaction. It was here, within the cage, waiting. Moving closer through the snow, the wolfling could smell the stale blood, hear the soft sighing of the animal's breathing. It was pretending to sleep, but the wolfling knew that for the lie it was. Blood was singing in its veins, its muscles preparing to attack. *Fool!* the wolfling thought, projecting its contempt. *Not yet . . .*

Then the cougar opened its eyes and hissed at the wolfling. It sprang swiftly to its feet and charged across the cage. With amused contempt, the wolfling stood its ground, sneering as the mountain lion stopped short, frustrated by the implacable metal bars that confined it. Furious, frustrated, it growled, then roared.

Enough! the wolfling ordered. The humans might be alerted by this howling. It moved to the cage, studying it, blatantly ignoring the challenging snarls the cougar was hurling its way. The frustrated cat was prowling up and down the tiny cage, wanting to be out, to attack.

Relax, the wolfling thought. *Soon, you will be free.* It examined the locking mechanism. Too complicated for any subtle maneuverings. And too strong for the mountain lion to ever break. But the wolfling was much, much stronger. . . . Glaring at the lock, the wolfling tensed its muscles, concentrating, feeling the power in each sinew, the strength of each claw. Then, in a swift move, with a deep snarl, it lashed out. Screeching claws raked the metal, and the lock was shattered. Carefully, the wolfling gripped the bars of the door and hauled backward.

With a low, moaning creak, the door pulled free of the upper hinge, swinging loosely in the dark. Chuckling with satisfaction, the wolfling dropped back to all fours and stared at the cougar. Slow and dim-witted it might be, but the animal had clearly realized that the wolfling was no normal challenger.

Come out, the wolfling told it. *Come out and play. Come out and die . . .*

Warily, the cougar moved toward the open, swinging door. Puzzled, it bared its teeth, snarling a low challenge. The wolfling, amused, barked out a response.

A blur of fangs, claws, and muscles, the cougar leaped at the wolfling. With almost weary contempt, the wolfling sprang aside, lashing out lazily as it moved. With its claws untensed, the blow it dealt the mountain lion hurt, but didn't draw blood. The wolfling couldn't afford blood just yet—the smell of hot blood would certainly overpower its control and send it into a feeding frenzy.

The mountain lion, smarting from the blow, dropped back into the snow. It looked at the wolfling and considered its next move. Fight or flight? The classic dilemma for all living creatures. To help it decide, the wolfling raised its front legs and made a show of tensing its claws. In the dim light, there was the barest gleam from their razor-sharp tips. Then the wolfling grinned, all teeth and promise of death.

The cougar turned and fled, a blur of tan fur against the white snow and black night. Forcing itself to wait, the wolfling let the animal get a head start before beginning the chase. Then, muscles rippling beneath its fur, the creature sprang and loped after the cougar.

The hunt was on!

The wolfling knew that the cougar had no notion of the layout of the game farm. It had known only the confines of the cage for several years. Within the grounds, the hunt would be too short, too simple. It wouldn't be fun; it would just be slaughter.

First things first, then. The cougar would be simple to find when the wolfling wanted it. Leaving it for now, the wolfling headed for the main exit. The eight-foot wall was no challenge for the wolfling, but the cougar would never make it. It would need an easier way out.

Reaching the main exit, it paused and watched. No sign of any keeper. The gate was locked, with a bar thrown across the back of the fencing. The wolfling snorted in contempt. Not even a challenge! It padded across the open ground, sniffing and listening for the approach of any human. Nothing. The bar across the back of the gate barely resisted the thrust of the wolfling's muscles, and then one blow from its massive paws snapped the lock clean through. A gentle push opened the gate sufficiently for the cougar to slip through. Excellent.

Turning around, the wolfling slipped back

through the darkness. Even if it couldn't smell the cougar, it would know where it was from the odor of fear the deer were giving off. The fool . . . it had its chance at freedom, and it simply wanted to kill. Cutting across the grounds, the wolfling loped along, heading to intercept. After a few moments, there was the scent and the silhouette in the drifting snow.

Hissing and spitting like any common household cat, the mountain lion turned to face the wolfling. Snarling in contempt, the wolfling bared its claws again and sprang. Used to being the attacker, not the victim, the cougar paused for a second. The wolfling's steel-hard claws slashed across its flank, leaving four trails of bright, warm blood. The cougar howled in pain and spun around to face the wolfling. The scent of fresh blood almost made the wolfling dizzy. It was like being drunk. Its long tongue rasped across its huge fangs, thirsty for the taste of the blood in its throat. A low growl of pleasure escaped its throat.

The cougar suddenly realized that it was looking at its own death. Panicking at last, it twisted around and ran off swiftly into the darkness. Right toward the main gate, as the wolfling had planned. Fighting down the urge to overtake and slay it, the wolfling ran behind the animal, issuing low, hungry growls from time to time to keep the terrified cougar fleeing in the right direction. The scent of blood was strong in the night air.

Then, abruptly, there was the gleam of a flashlight beam. For a second, the wolfling was blinded, and it cursed its own stupidity. It had let the intoxication of the chase, the smell of the blood, go to its head, and had forgotten to be careful. One of the keepers had again braved the weather to check on the animals.

The cougar, seizing the chance the distraction offered, ran for the gate and out into the night. The keeper hadn't even spotted it. All of his attention was riveted on the huge, snarling form centered in his flashlight beam. The human seemed frozen in shock, unable to take in the reality of a wolf this size, this unusual, this other-worldly.

There was no option now. The wolfling surrendered all rational thought, and fell back on to its instincts. With a howl that split the night, it leaped for the keeper. The foolish human barely had a chance to scream and throw up his hands, a weak defense against the powerful jaws and slashing claws that ripped into him . . .

Dizzily, the wolfling regained its feet, the heavy stickiness of human blood dripping from its muzzle. Shaking its head to clear the blood-lust, it managed finally to focus on the gate ahead. Somewhere off in the darkness there was the slamming of doors, and then more lights dancing in the night. The urge to howl was too strong to deny, and then the wolfling was off again, darting for the gate and freedom in the anonymity of the night.

Running helped to clear its head. Slowly, the thundering power of the blood-lust receded, and the wolfling could think again. It was too late to be concerned about the human. The others would find the cougar missing and assume that the killing was its work. They would never know of the wolfling. Its one regret was that it didn't have more time to have enjoyed the killing. There was no satisfaction in what it had done. It had been too simple, too swift.

Its head clear again, the wolfling cast about for the scent of the cougar. There, off to the east! It was heading for the hills, as the wolfling had hoped. Good . . . there would be a fine hunt this night after all. The mountain lion might think that it was free, but it wasn't.

Two

As the alarm screeched shrilly in his ear, Cory Darnell floundered about, striking out with his left arm from under the tangle of his bed sheets. Finally, mostly through luck, he hit the snooze bar, and the irritating sound stopped hammering at his sensitive ears. Then he let his arm flop tiredly down, and considered the possibility of actually waking up.

His head hurt, his body ached, and he felt pretty certain his eyeballs would prove to be fried and useless—if he could ever pry his eyelids open. It must have been some party the night before.

His thoughts gradually began to assemble from the scattered recesses of his shattered mind. It was Monday morning, and time he was up, getting ready for school. The previous day

—yeah, Sunday, that was it—he had helped the team to its latest win. And against Bannock High, no less, last year's champions. Then . . . then what? He struggled to recall. There had been the suggestion of a party, and he remembered agreeing to it. After that, nothing.

Man, how much did he have to drink? He knew he wasn't supposed to hit the beers, but everyone else did, and they had never affected him before, except for that great buzzed feeling. He must have really thrown a few back if he felt this bad.

The alarm started screaming at him again. Determined this time, he hauled at the sheets until his head was free. He tried opening his eyes, but the daylight burned so brightly that he hastily screwed them shut again. Aiming for the sound, he kept slapping until he managed to hit the snooze bar again.

Right, try again to get up. He was face down, so first he tried to roll over. He almost yelled aloud from the pain that arced through his chest muscles and down to his fingertips. His fuzzy head was bad enough, but what was going on here? Steeling himself to the pain, he pushed hard and flopped over onto his back, breathing heavily. Gradually, as he rested, the agony that had knotted his muscles calmed down, and he could start to think without sharp pains hacking at his sensitive brain.

He'd never felt like this before. Not even that time he'd had almost two six-packs and gotten so drunk that he'd come home to the wrong house and fallen into the Murphy's pool. He'd woken up the next morning with a splitting head and a sensitive stomach—and on the receiving end of a brutal lecture from his father. But now . . . he really felt terrible. Every move set his muscles on fire. Maybe he'd just lie here a while and—

The alarm started howling again. This alone gave him the energy to swing upright, reach over, and attempt to murder the sadistic little clock. He finally settled for just shutting it off, since he lacked the strength to throw it through the open window as he had intended.

Open window? This close to Christmas? He couldn't remember opening it, but that *did* explain why his room felt so cold. Maybe it explained why he felt so sore, too. He might have caught a chill. Bummer. That could really ruin his playing for the rest of the season.

Now that he was sitting up, the red splotches in front of his aching eyes seemed to be dying away. His breathing was a little less ragged, and the pain across his shoulders was working its way back down to being merely unbearable. Taking a deep breath, he staggered uncertainly to his feet. The room seemed to spin around, and he stumbled rather than walked over to the window. Resting there, he waited for his strength to return. He dimly saw the crisp snow outside, and realized that there were footprints in it leading to his window.

He slammed it closed, then leaned against it, waiting for his muscles to stop twisting and hurting. Footprints outside . . . what time had he come home? It must have been pretty late, if he'd sneaked in the back way to avoid waking his folks. What had he been up to at the celebration party that left him like this?

Finally, he felt strong enough to try to make it across his room and to the bathroom. A shower would clear his head and help his aches. He opened his eyes again and looked around. The bedroom was its usual mess; he'd never managed to develop the neat habits his parents seemed to think essential for him. Various items of clothing were scattered over the bed, desk, and dresser. Books and papers flowed from the desk to the floor, and were currently making a determined assault on his stereo. CDs were piled on top of the stereo, on the dresser, and some were over on the night table. One of the posters—the Penn State lineup—had lost a pin and the corner had folded forward, flapping erratically. His closet door was only half-closed, and the wreckage in there was even worse.

Well, at least his room was normal, even if he wasn't.

He made it across to the mirror on the back of his door and paused to examine the damage. He was a shade under six feet tall and a hundred and eighty pounds—all muscle, and he was proud of that. Every ounce of power went into his tackles, which is why he was the all-time best linebacker Branton High had ever fielded. He worked hard to stay in shape, and had a thick, powerful frame. He ran a large hand through his tangle of sandy hair, and as his eyes focused more, he started to shake.

He'd gone to bed in just his shorts, as usual, and his chest was bare. He began to see why it was hurting so much.

There was a crisscrossing of welts all over it, and small trails of dried blood. It was as if someone or something had actually clawed at his naked chest. And pretty deeply in places, too. How the heck had that happened? It did explain some of the agony in the muscles—but not all. It felt like every muscle in his body had been bent out of shape somehow and was still trying to get back to normal. He fingered the wounds on his chest, puzzled.

This must have happened last night. And, presumably, he'd had his shirt off at the time. In the middle of winter? Boy, he must have really been out of his head! He tried to think. What shirt was he wearing last night? Right, the orange sweatshirt. He glanced around the room and saw it tossed on to the chair by the desk. Moving slowly to minimize the pain, he crossed to it and picked the shirt up.

It was coverd in blood.

He stood there for a moment, holding it, unable to understand. There was no way this could all be his own blood. Despite the cuts on his chest, he hadn't really bled too much, or his sheets would have been soaked, too. So—where —or *who?*—had the rest of the blood come from?

He knew he should start feeling scared, but he hurt far too much to be able to work up a panic. Had he gotten into a fight? Beaten someone up? He couldn't remember. He could recall the game perfectly, the final victory. Then he'd showered and left with Rob, Mark, and the rest for the party. And then—nothing.

No, not quite nothing. It hurt him to do it, but he concentrated on the fuzzy memories dancing on the edge of his mind. Finally, one of them became a little clearer. An animal, in the night. All teeth and growling . . .

A mountain lion. Yeah, that was it. A cougar.

What? What the hell was he thinking about? There weren't any mountain lions anywhere near Branton. This was crazy. But his memory insisted: there had been one, last night. He could see it vividly, etched in his mind's eye. It was backed into a tree, snarling and spitting, and terrified as it hissed its hatred at him. Then, a kind of red haze, and suddenly the animal was dead, and he was there, on his knees in the snow, its blood and fur all over him. There was the heavy, sweet smell of hot blood, and a vague memory of lapping at it . . .

With a cry, he wrenched his mind back to the room, feeling dizzy. Swaying, he threw the bloody shirt away from him. Then, stung by a thought, he realized he'd have questions to answer if the shirt was found. Questions he couldn't answer. It was hard to concentrate, and the only place he could think of hiding it was under his bed. Hastily, he managed to get down on his knees and push the bloody memento as far under as he could reach.

He felt sick again. The bathroom. As he made his way to the door, he grabbed his robe.

Jenny almost always beat him to the bathroom in the morning, and today she could have gone there via the mall and still beaten him. The last thing he needed was for her to see him all scratched up and to start making a scene about it. Kid sisters should either be outlawed or else simply hung at birth. At ten years old, Jenny had decided she was her own person, and that the best way to prove it was to try to embarrass her heroic older brother in every way she possibly could.

After two attempts, he managed to get both arms into different sleeves of his robe and drew it tightly around him. Then he made his way out into the hall. As he feared, the bathroom door was locked. Hammering on the wood, he yelled: "Come on, move it in there!"

"Go pick your boogers!" Jenny called back. "I was here first."

He didn't even have the strength to argue with her. Leaning against the wall, he closed his eyes and sighed. It was definitely going to be a long day.

A few minutes later the door opened, and Jenny glared at him. She had to look up a long way, since she was only four feet eight, but she managed to put all of her ten-year-old's contempt into her voice. "It's all yours. And make

305

sure you use your own toothbrush this morning."

"Okay," he agreed. "I will. I used yours to clean the toilet last night."

Before she could think of a snappy comeback to this, he slammed the door in her face and locked it. Then he stumbled for the shower.

By the time he went downstairs for breakfast, Cory felt a lot better. Now he just wanted to sleep instead of die. And he was beginning to get his thoughts into better shape. It was stupid to have even thought that he could possibly have seen a mountain lion last night, let alone killed one. As for lapping up its warm blood . . . he shuddered and managed to snatch the orange juice carton from Jenny before she took the last bit. She made a face at him and dove for the pancakes.

Luckily, their mom chose that moment to come back into the kitchen. "Jennifer Ann!" she snapped. "Stop picking on your brother."

Jenny frowned. "You're always on his side."

"Only when you're in the wrong. Cory needs his food today, after his performance yesterday."

Cory belatedly realized his mother was referring to the football game, and he grinned sheepishly. At the same time, he scooped several pancakes onto his plate before Jenny could try again.

"Big deal," Jenny commented. "So he can kick a ball around a field and beat up on guys smaller than him. So what?"

"So we're all proud of him," their father said, coming in. He punched Cory affectionately on the arm and Cory bit back a scream of pain. "Way to go, champ. I'll bet you get that offer from Perdue. Or maybe Penn State." He grinned again. "My son, the college star."

"Stop pressuring him, dear," Cory's mother said. She fixed her earrings, and scooped up her car keys on the way to the garage. As always, she was smartly dressed in a dark suit. "See you later. Love you all." Then she was gone, ready for another day at the bank.

"Hey, it's not pressure!" Dad called to her, after she was gone. He turned and winked at Cory. "No pressure, right? Just a future grid star!"

Cory managed a weak smile. "Right," he agreed, drowning the pancakes in maple syrup.

"So what am I?" Jenny complained. "Chopped liver?"

"Certainly not," her father said, bending to

kiss her cheek. "You just inherited your mother's brains, instead of my brawn."

"Yeah," she agreed. "The brains sure skipped Cory."

"Jen," Dad said warningly. He glanced at the clock. "Grief! Look at the time." He clicked on the radio. "I'll get the latest traffic report, then I'm outta here!"

The announcer was just finishing an item about a school budget hearing. Then, changing the mood, she went on: "There was an animal escape from the Crystal Brook Game Farm last night, that left a keeper dead. Somehow, a mountain lion broke out of its cage, struck down keeper George Zukorski, and then escaped into the night. Police are beginning a hunt for the creature, which remains at large. Sheriff Ben Oliphant told this station that though the mountain lion has killed, he doesn't believe it to be a danger to the community. It headed for the hills, and should be captured shortly. He does suggest, however, that anyone venturing into the Crystal Springs area takes extra care. And now the traffic—"

Cory heard nothing after that. His hands were shaking so hard that he dropped his fork with a clatter. He stuck his hands under the table to hide them. Jenny was too busy stuffing her face to notice, and his dad was taking in the snarls in the traffic.

There really was a mountain lion! Cory thought. It had escaped last night and killed someone. Once again, he saw, quite vividly, himself facing the creature as it spat at him in fear. Then, less clearly, he saw the animal dead, and himself stooping to the body . . .

No, it was impossible! There was no way that he could have killed a full-grown mountain lion, especially not if he had been out partying. And, anyway, the reporter hadn't said that the lion was dead. It was crazy to think that he might have had anything to do with the animal.

But . . . what about those claw marks that stung under the antiseptic on his chest?